Cucumber Quest 2

The Ripple Kingdom

Gigi D.G.

First Second
New York

CHAPTER 1
Disaster in Paradise

Ugh...
Huh?

Almond?
Sir Carrot?
Are you h—
whoa!
SKKKK

KKKK

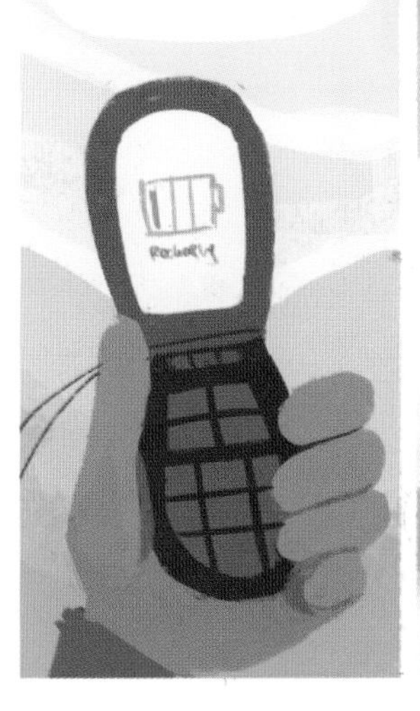
Is this a...

Nooo!

Please, you have to believe me!
It's the truth! I swear it!
Yeah, and I'm Queen Conch, toots!
If you'd only allow me to speak with your boss, I could—
Nobody sees the boss without gettin' by us, see?
Nobody gets by us without a reservation, see?
And YOU don't got one, see?

But I'm—
And you know what happens to kids what don't got reservations?
They get a clippin', see?
Yeah! A clippin'!
Yeah!
A clippin'!
Yeah!
Yeah!
Yeah!
clip
clip
snip
clip
clip
clip
snip
clack
EEEK!
Nooo, don't!
I just got this dress!
clack
clip
clip
clack
clip
clack
clip
clip
Someone—anyone, HELP!!

Hey!
You should, um...
You should stop that!
What's **your** problem, kid?
well i just
um
Tongue-tied, eh? Clip him, boys!
Uh-oh!
scuttle
scuttle
scuttle
scuttle
scuttle
scuttle
scuttle
scuttle

BOOM

YOW! This kid's playin' with fire!
Let's scram, boys!
scuttle
scuttle
scuttle
scuttle
Wow. I can't believe that actually worked.
gasp
You saved me!
Thank you so much!
I-It was nothing! I couldn't just stand by and watch.

Please, my brave hero, won't you tell me your name?

I'm Cucumber, but I'm not really a h—

Sea... cucumber...?

N-No, Cucumber Cucumber! I'm from the Doughnut Kingdom.

Oh! Then welcome to the Ripple Kingdom, Not-Sea Cucumber!

My name is Princess Nautilus. It's a pleasure to meet you!

Y-You're **the** princess?! Wow!
Oh, but please just call me Nautilus.
Okay!
Oh, or how about I call you Nautie for sh—
...how about i call you nautilus.
That would be wonderful!
So what brings you to this country, Cucumber?
Well, my friends and I came looking for a legendary sword, but our ship sank...
Legendary sword?
Cucumber...

Oh my goodness, **of course!**
You must be a descendant of the legendary hero who defeated the Nightmare Knight!
That's what everyone's been saying...
You seem to know a lot, though!
Of course I do!!
In case of the Nightmare Knight's return, my family has preserved knowledge from ancient times in order to aid the hypothetical new hero in his quest.
I've spent my **whole life** studying the legends for this opportunity!
Oh, wow!
You know, I kind of like reading about this stuff, too—
No, Cucumber.

You don't understand.
I live "this stuff."
I breathe "this stuff."
I know the legend of the Nightmare knight better than I know what I had for breakfast this morning!
That's—
And it's even more important now that he's been revived.
Terrible things are already happening in our kingdom!
Just getting here was pretty terrible.
This giant squid monster came out of nowhere—
GASP!
You mean Splashmaster?

Huh?
That's that horrible thing's name!
He's one of the Disaster Masters!
...Huh?
Y...
You mean nobody's told you yet?!
ehe he ehe ehehehehehehe hehe he
Lend me your ear, O Legendary Hero, and I shall tell you of the foul beings that once terrorized our land!
For such is my second-greatest duty as princess of the Ripple Kingdom!
What's the first—
Shh! All things in due time, Hero! My gosh!!
I'm sorry!

ahem
Many, many years ago...
The seven kingdoms of Dreamside lived in peace and harmony.
But one day, the Nightmare Knight appeared to shatter that peace.
With his great and terrible power...
he cast our world into an age of darkness that threatened to last forever.

The Nightmare Knight created seven monsters and appointed them to rule over the conquered kingdoms of Dreamside.
They came to be known as the Disaster Masters, and each one was more powerful than the last.
The first was Splashmaster.
The second was...
uh...
Um...
...I'm sorry.
I can't seem to remember any of the rest.
H-How long did you say you were studying this again?

But I do remember that they're very nasty and they need to be taken care of.

And if you're going to do battle with Splashmaster...

then it's my destiny to go with you!

Huh? Is that really okay?

Certainly!

Now that my second-most important duty is complete, it's time for the first!

Oh! So what was that, after all?

Heck if I remember!

And it's a shame, too. I get the feeling it was **really** important.

Well, I'm sure it'll come to me sooner or later.

Oh, but first!
I hate to ask for your help again so soon, but there's something I'm looking for.
What's that?
I'm sure you've noticed, but this area is home to the Crabsters.
Just that way is the Crabster Resort.
The owner is a friend of mine, and I know he'll be able to help me get back home...
but the guards you saw earlier don't believe I'm really the princess, so they won't let me in.
Luckily, I've been trained in the royal art of summoning.
If I can just call my familiar, that **should** be all the proof I need...
but when I washed ashore here, I lost my Royal Instrument of Summoning, and I can't seem to find it anywhere.
Oh, that's too bad.

Well, I don't know anything about your summoning thing...
...but I did find this cell phone.
Maybe we can use it to call for hel—
GASP
That's it!!
My Royal Instrument of Summoning!
Th-This? But it's a cell pho—
YOINK
It's not a cell phone, Cucumber.
It's a Royal Instrument of Summoning that's been passed down through my family for generations.
i'm sorry.

With this, I can prove my identity to the guards!
Let's go!
a-HEM!
so i says to her, i says—
Ex-CUSE me, sirs.
I emphatically request that you allow me a meeting with the owner of this establishment.
Hey, you're that seashell dame!
Got sand in those ears, doll? No reservation, no entry!
Maybe we oughta pencil you in for a clippin' instead, see?

There will be no clipping!
I didn't think it would come to this, but if you still refuse to believe my words, then I have no choice!
beep
boop
Behold, gentlemen!
The proof of my royal heritage!
caw
caw
Come, Liquus!
I summon thee!

WHOOOSHH
flop
WHOOOOOAAAAAAA
Did you see that?!
This dame **is** the princess!
wha
Wait there a minute, got it?

Oh... I'm sorry, Liquus.
I should have known you'd still be tired out from earlier.
Earlier?
Splashmaster attacked the Ocean Palace earlier and tried to kidnap me.
I knew I had to escape...
... so I summoned Liquus to give him a nasty shock!
And he let you go? Wow!
I was carried away by the waves, and I ended up so far from home...
...but it must have been destiny if I ended up meeting you, Cucumber!
Uh–
CREE

Our apologies for the wait, madam and sir.
Please, come in.

This place is amazing!
I vacationed here all the time when I was younger.
It's good to see it hasn't changed!

When will we be able to meet with the owner?
The master is presently occupied, madam.
Please relax in the lobby until he is available.
Isn't this wonderful, Cucumber?
With the Crabsters' help, we'll be on our way in no time!

Huh?
O-Oh, uh— yeah!
Hey, wait up!

creeeeakkkkk...
Huh?
Where the heck...?

ME HOOOME!
EEEEEEK!!
!!
SMASHD BUNY HOWS
ccreeeakkk
ME BEAT OLD RECORD SOON!

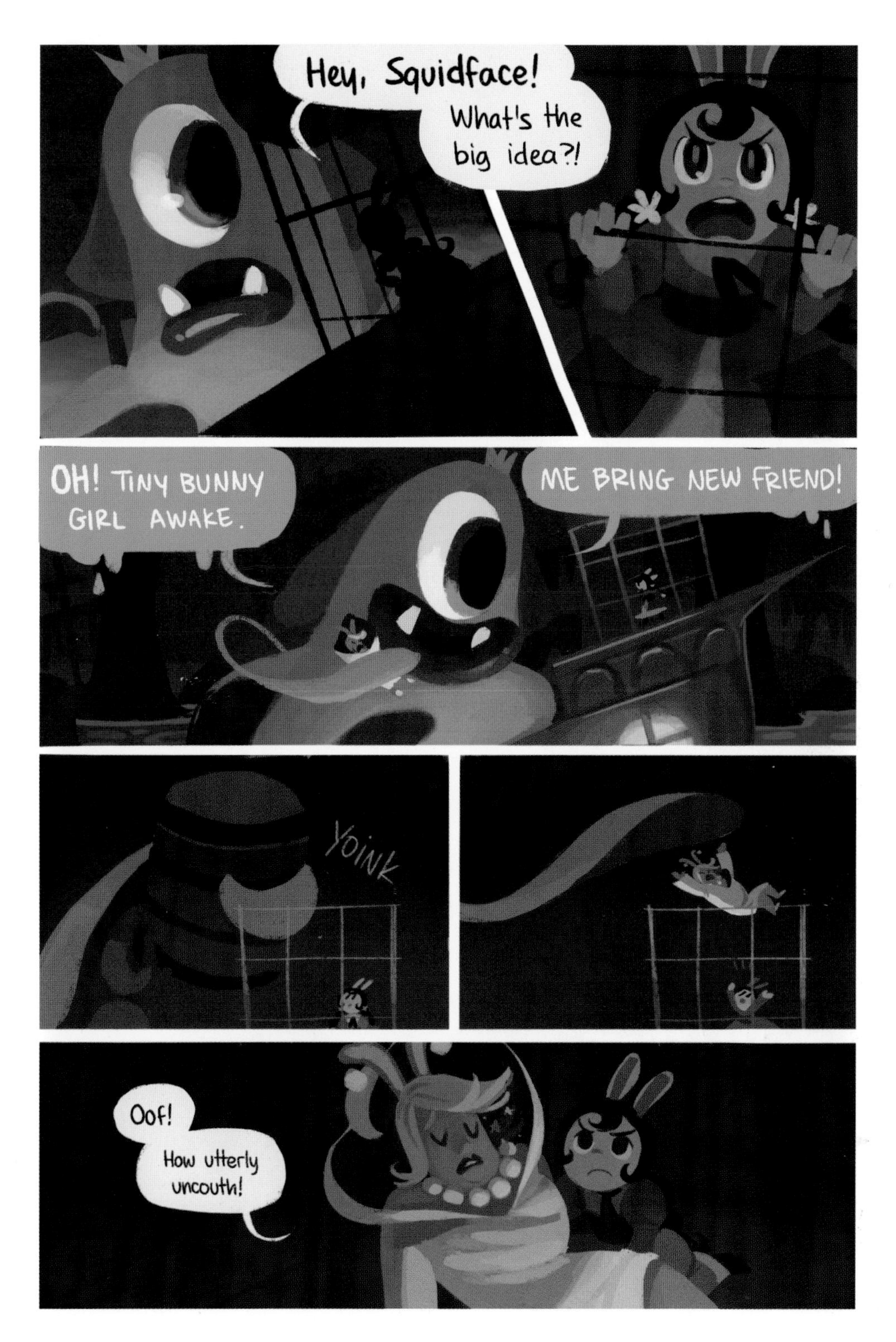
Hey, Squidface!
What's the big idea?!
OH! TINY BUNNY GIRL AWAKE.
ME BRING NEW FRIEND!
YOINK
Oof!
How utterly uncouth!

What'd you do with my brother and Carrot, you jerk?!
BWUH?
OHH!
TINY BUNNY FRIENDS. ME THINK THEY DROWN.
No way!
Once I get out of here and find them, you're getting a world-class slaying!
HUH HUH HUH!
TRY, BUT BUNNY GIRL TOO WEAK TO MOVE BARREL!
We'll SEE who's too weak once I beat your slimy face in!
HUH HUH HUH
Splashmaster.

It is time for your report, Splashmaster.

But first...

What is that ridiculous thing on your head?

LIMBO KING

ME GET PRIZE FOR SMASH BUNNYMAN BOAT!
NOW ME LOOK LIKE KING!
YOU LIKE?
n-no like?
...Wear it if you must. Just report.

GOOD TIME! ME CATCH LOTS OF TINY BUNNYMANS TODAY.
Which "tiny bunnymans"?
ME GET PRINCESS LIKE YOU SAY!
Good.
Show her to me.
OK!
EEEEEK!!
HERE YOU GOOOO!

This is the queen.
...SO
So, it is not the princess.
They are two different people.
Surely even you can grasp such a basic concept.
BUT QUEEN JUST OLDER, FATTER PRINCESS.
I BEG YOUR PARDON?!
...

You have failed me again, Splashmaster.
But perhaps I should have known better than to expect you to follow simple instructions.
ME SORRY.
...BUT ME DO BETTER!
PRINCESS NO BIG DEAL. ME CATCH HERO ALREADY!
...Interesting.
Very well. Show me this hero you have captured.
OK!!

UGH!!

This girl?

Is the hero not a young boy by the name of Cucumber?

That's my big brother. Not like **he's** much of a hero, anyway!

I see.

And tell me, Splashmaster...
Of what use to me is the legendary hero's little sister?
W—
UGHHH!! Enough already!
I'm SO SICK of everyone brushing me off!
Listen, Nightmare Knight: I may not be as old as my big brother...
but I can still beat you up!!
Really.
eventually

You have failed me again, Splashmaster.
Again.
ME SORRY.
Then waste no more of my time.
The hero is sure to come here in search of his sister.
When he does, eliminate him.
OK...
My patience is wearing thin. Do not disappoint me again.

Why did it take you so long to call?!

Sorry, Mom!

I've been worried sick ever since Almond ran off on her own!

... But I guess I shouldn't have expected that girl to stay put.

That's Almond for you.

So how's the quest going? I want to hear everything!

but there was this big squid monster on the way, and—

Oh!

Don't tell me all the scary details, sweetheart! You know how worried I am!
Okay, I guess...
But you seemed so excited about this before.
Oh, you know how parents are, dear.
Sometimes we just rush our kids out the door because it's so hard to say goodbye!
I... think you're the only parent who does that, Mom.
It was all very spur of the moment, honey. I'm sure even your father is up all night worrying about you two!
I'M BRISKET SWEATS AND I'M HERE AT THE LEMON BAR & GRILL IN CAKETOWN WHERE I'M ABOUT TO TAKE ON THE "ARCHITECTURAL DIGEST" CHALLEN
I doubt it, Mom.
CHIPS

Well, as long as you two are safe, that's all I need to hear.
Can you put Almond on for a second, sweetie?
Uh
she's
G...Gee, you know what— I think she **just** ran off somewhere! S-Sorry!
Your Highness? Mister Cucumber?
Oh? That's too bad.
The master is now available to see you.
Oh!
A-Anyway, I gotta go!
Well, all right, honey. You kids take care of each other, okay?
We will! Bye!
click

You know...
I still don't get why we couldn't just use your ph— Royal Instrument for that.
Cucumber, please. Listen to yourself.
This way, please...
Sir, there are guests here to see you.
Guests?
What'd I tell ye about bringin' in uninvited guests?!

Captain Bubblebeard? Is that you?
Yarr?
Well, shiver me timbers!
If it isn't Princess Nautilus!
Well met, Captain! It's been so long!
Aye! Haven't seen ye in a whale's age!

And who've ye brought with ye?
This is Cucumber, the legendary hero!
Actually—
Yarr! Glad to hear it!
Beggin' yer pardon fer the rough welcome, Princess.
Shipwrecked?
I've got me claws full takin' care o' all these shipwrecked tourists!
Aye! Nasty, squiddly beast called Splashmaster made a mess o' their vacation.
Splashmaster!
Captain, that's the reason I'm here!
What's that, lass?

He's one of the Nightmare Knight's henchmen! He tried to kidnap me!
Kidnap ye?! The nerve!
Can you do anything to stop him, Captain?
O'course!
Back in me younger days, ol' Bubblebeard was feared across the seven seas!
I'll find that beast and tie its tentacles in a knot, I will!
Wow!!
...is what I'd be sayin' if I didn't settle down to open me resort.
I got no strength fer fightin' anymore.
Me heart's in me business!
Oh. W-Well, that's okay.

We'll just have to take care of him ourselves!
Seafoam City is in danger as long as he's around...
I need to get back there to make sure my mother and father are all right!
Noble as ever, Princess! Brings a tear ter me eye!
And if ye be wantin' a trip back home, I'll do that much for ye!
You'll show us the way?

More'n that!
I'll toss ye right over there meself!
Wow!

Isn't that great, Nautil—
... Nautilus?

Nautilus!
43rd ANNUAL LIMBO-THON
How low!
Can you go!
Oh yeah! We've got a new limbo King here, everybody!
Or should I say... limbo queen!
Let's hear it for her!
Woo!
yeah!
Thank you!
Thank you, my loyal limbo subjects!
We'd normally have a big crown trophy to give our champ, but, uh...
We kinda lost it when the ship sank. Sorry!
Oh! What a pity.

ahem!
Nautilus?
Oh!
You'll have to forgive me, Cucumber.
It looked like so much fun, and I couldn't help myself.
bye!
sigh
Yarr!
One Seafoam City voyage, comin' up!
Climb aboard!
Uh—
CLACK

Are ye ready, kids?
Aye aye, Captain!
I can't heeear youuuu
Aye aye, Captain!
OHHHHHHHH
Uh, wait!
When you said you'd "toss us over," you didn't literally—
AAAAAAAAA
BOMBS AWAY!
ding!
Yer welcooome!

aaaaaaaaaaaaaaa
AAAAAAAAA
Pffffff
This is...

Wow!
This must be Coral Canyon!
I can't believe the captain managed to throw us this far!
I thought we were going to Seafoam City.
Oh, well, that's right nearby!
All we need to do is continue through the canyon, cross Seastar Lagoon...
... reach the northern island, and enter the ocean caves!
Th...That's not nearby at all!
Chin up, Cucumber! Exercise is good for the body and spirit!
I guess so...
I just hope there aren't any surprises along—
heyyyyy!

Did you hear that just now?
Hm?
Hear wha—
BONK
OW OW OW OW OW
GASP
Oh no!!
I'm so sorry! I should have been more careful!
I-It's all right.
Was that you calling us just now?
Oh! Yes, it was!

You're Cucumber, aren't you? The legendary hero?
...
I guess?
Great! My name is Chardonnay, and I serve the Dream Oracle.
There's something very important I need to tell you!
A servant of the Dream Oracle herself?!
How amazing!
I can only imagine what it's like to work for her!
scritch
scritch
scritch
S-So, um, what did you come to tell us?
Oh!

Legendary Hero, please listen carefully.
To defeat the Nightmare Knight, you must first deal with all seven of his underlings.
They're called the Disaster Masters, and—
Oh, don't worry! I told him about them already.
Kinda.
You did?
Phew! That saves me an explanation.
We just need to make sure every hero is clear on this stuff, you know?
Haha, yeah...
Wait, what?
Eep!

Did you just say "every"?
Um— Uhh—
Yes!
You and the first hero!
See? Every one!
Tee hee!
Chardonnay?
How many times has the Nightmare Knight been resurrected?
H-How many?!
W-Well, just once!
... every ... 5,000 years or so...
Huh?

But according to my studies, the legend is 500,000 years old!
Then, that means...
He's been resurrected 100 times?
This... would be 100.
Yes.
And when were you planning to tell me that?!
OH NOOOO
HEROES FOR GENERATIONS
You're freaking out! I knew you'd freak out!
Of course I'm freaking out!
A HUNDRED TIMES?!
I thought he was KIDDING!

I'm sorry! I really am!
The truth is, the Nightmare Knight is immortal, so we can't **really** defeat him...
Keeping him sealed away with the Dream Sword is the best we can do.
How long does the seal last?
Oh, that's the good part! It lasts forever!
as long as nobody assembles the Disaster Stones
B-But we hide those all over Dreamside!
I mean, in places no one would **THINK** to look!
But they've been found.
100 times.
And it's **awful!!**

Every 5,000 years, there's always **SOMEBODY** who wants to take over Dreamside...
... and no matter what we do, they **ALWAYS** manage to find every Disaster Stone!
It's almost **SCARY** how good they are at it!
Huh...
Well, Saturday didn't seem to have any trouble finding one.
Where do you hide them?
COME

Please don't get mad! I'm trying my best!
We understand, Chardonnay! Don't cry!
But still, doesn't this make everything we're doing feel kind of...
pointless?
I mean, even if we beat the Nightmare Knight, he'll just be back in 5,000 years...
and 5,000 years after that...
We have to find a way to truly defeat him, Cucumber!
It's our responsibility to make sure future generations don't live under his shadow!
That **sounds** good...
But if 99 other heroes couldn't find a way to do it, how are **we** supposed to?
I... don't know yet.
But don't lose hope!
Captain Bubblebeard once told me that any problem will crack open if you never stop punching it!
It... probably helps to have fists as big as his.

I'm so sorry for discouraging you!
There has to be **something** we haven't tried,
so please don't give up yet, okay?
We'll make sure this 100th time is the last!
Or try, anyway.
It makes me happy to hear that kind of determination!
With the right attitude, I'm sure you can do it.
I need to return to the Oracle for now, but I'll be praying for your success!
Thank you, Chardonnay!
Take care!

Look, Sir Carrot!
The stars are so beautiful!
...I am 'appy you came to spend tonight watching them with moi.
W-Why, Princess, of course!
A moment spent without you would be a moment wasted.

There's something I've been meaning to ask you...
You okay, bro?
YAHHH!!

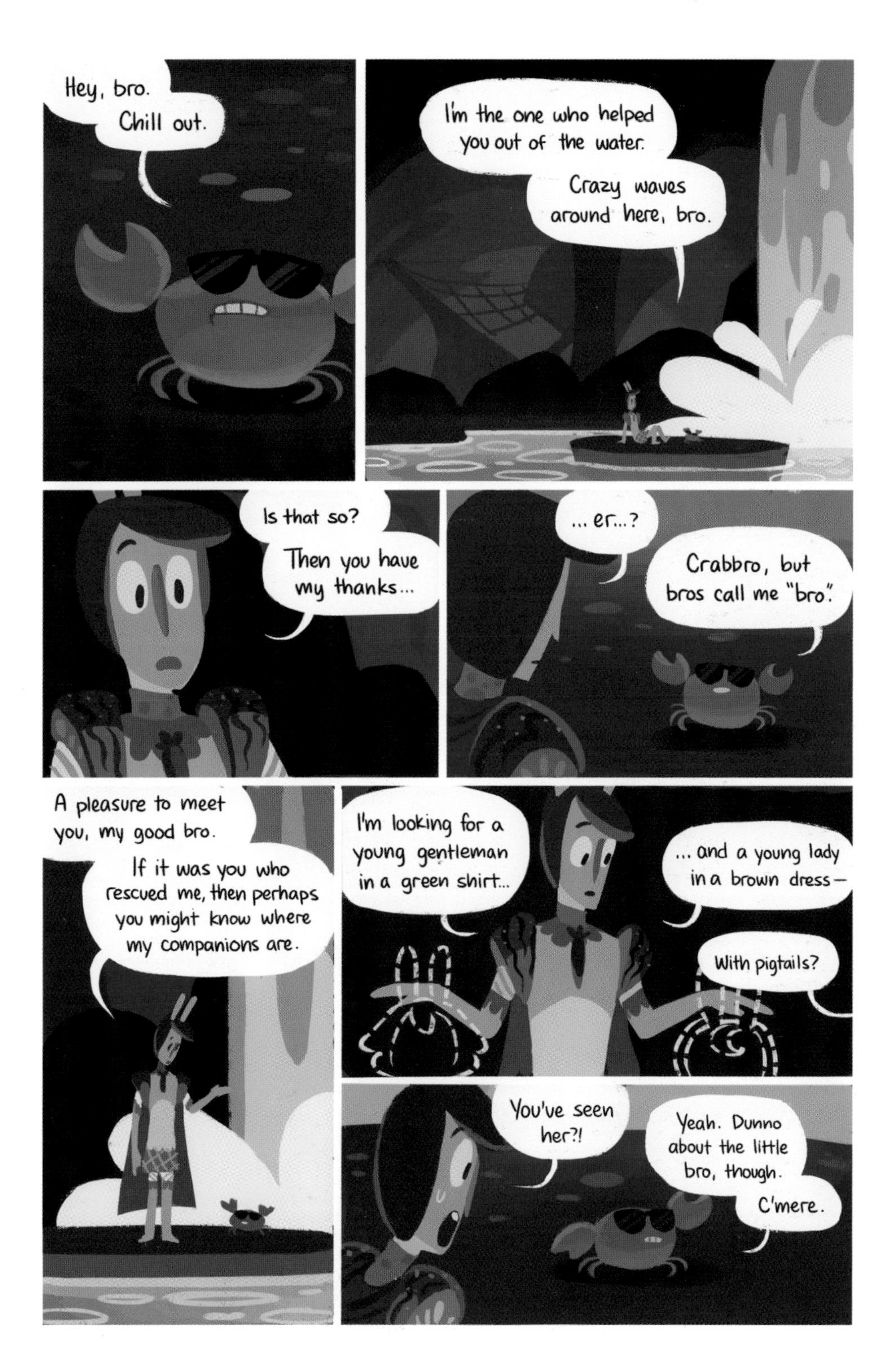
Hey, bro.
Chill out.
I'm the one who helped you out of the water.
Crazy waves around here, bro.
Is that so?
Then you have my thanks...
... er...?
Crabbro, but bros call me "bro".
A pleasure to meet you, my good bro.
If it was you who rescued me, then perhaps you might know where my companions are.
I'm looking for a young gentleman in a green shirt...
... and a young lady in a brown dress—
With pigtails?
You've seen her?!
Yeah. Dunno about the little bro, though.
C'mere.

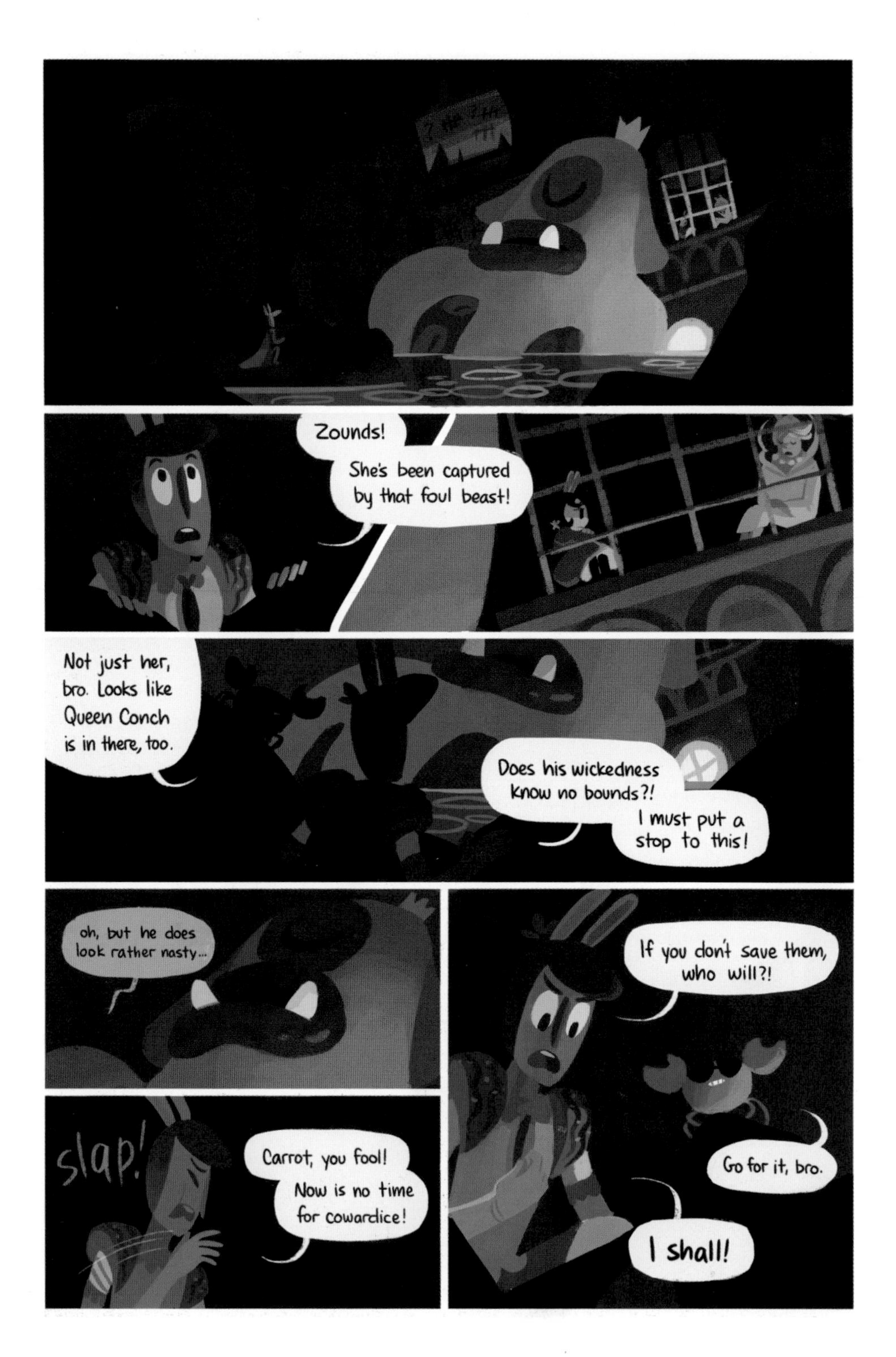

Zounds!
She's been captured by that foul beast!
Not just her, bro. Looks like Queen Conch is in there, too.
Does his wickedness know no bounds?!
I must put a stop to this!
oh, but he does look rather nasty...
slap!
Carrot, you fool!
Now is no time for cowardice!
If you don't save them, who will?!
Go for it, bro.
I shall!

Hear me, villain!
HUH?
Carrot?!
Your reign of terror is at its end!
I shall strike you dow—
erm

H-Hey!
Let go of that!!
NOOOOO
creeee
eeak

Cool moves.
I... have failed you.
Well, at least you tried.
That's better than Grizzlygum, I guess.
i suppose it is.
But now that both of us are in here...
All we can do...
...is wait for my big brother to come and pfffffhahahaha.
I can't even finish that.
Hey, if you're done moping, get over here and help me out.
I've got a plan...

We've made it, Cucumber!
Seastar Lagoon!
Isn't it beautiful?
And huge!
So many brilliant thinkers have visited this place to reflect on the mysteries of the universe!
Don't you feel enlightened just standing here?
N-Not really...

You aren't still depressed because of the Nightmare Knight, are you?
A little.
It's weird to know we're up against an enemy we can't really brrglrf
No negative talk, Cucumber.
We said we would find a way, remember?
yesh
I jusht wish we had a clue where Shaturday went with the Dream Shord.
That'd give ush shomething to shtart with, at leasht...

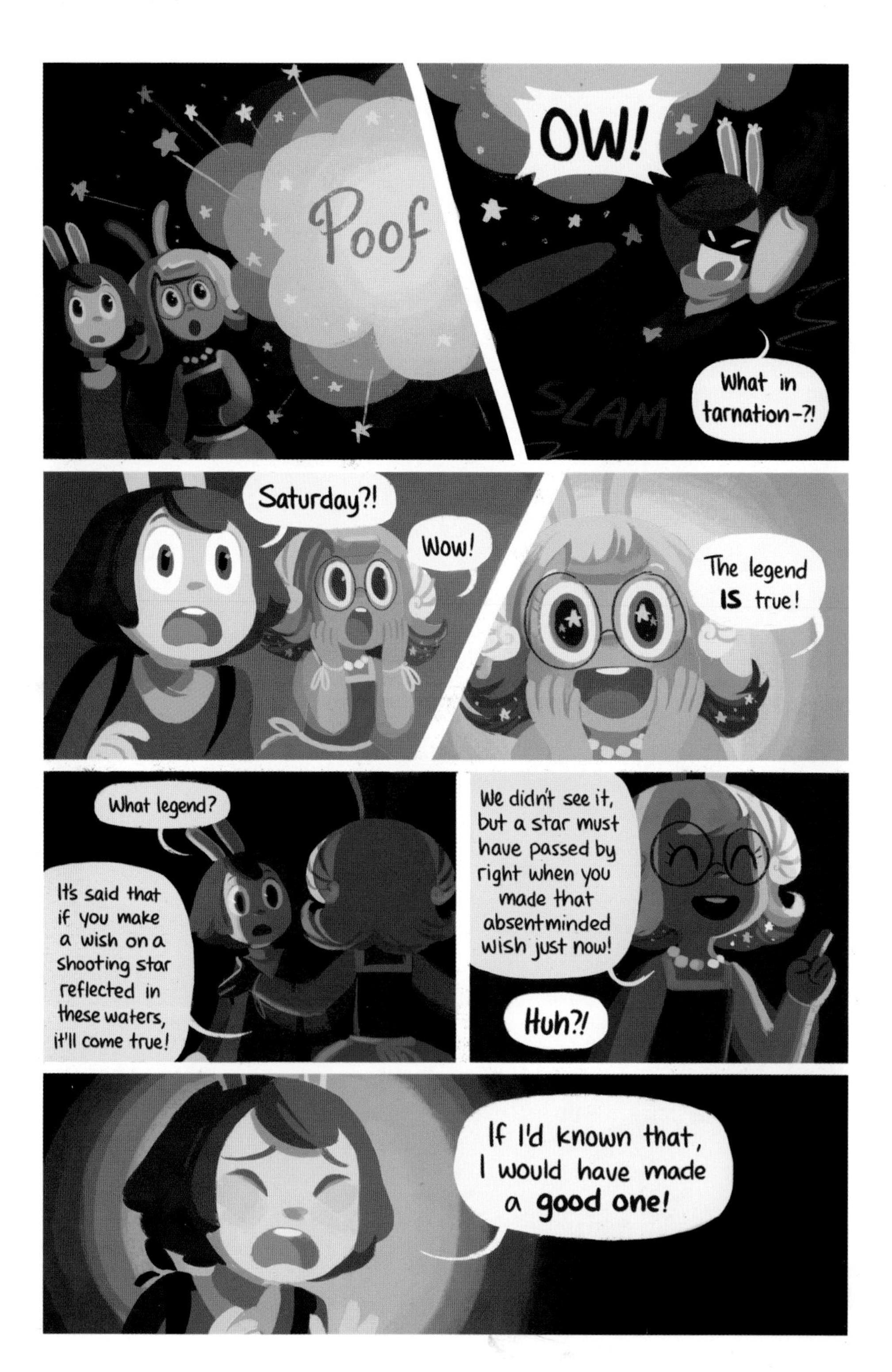
Poof
OW!
What in tarnation-?!
SLAM
Saturday?!
Wow!
The legend IS true!
What legend?
It's said that if you make a wish on a shooting star reflected in these waters, it'll come true!
We didn't see it, but a star must have passed by right when you made that absentminded wish just now!
Huh?!
If I'd known that, I would have made a good one!

I WISH ALMOND WERE HERE
I WISH I COULD GO HOME
Urgh...
Hey now!
Yer that kid from the Doughnut Kingdom, ain't ya!
The name is Cucumber!
Tell a gal who cares!
Where'n the heck am I, anyway?
Seastar Lagoon!
I, uh... I brought you here, I guess!
Now how in Dreamside'd ya do that?
W-Wish power, I guess?

Well, I hope yer plannin' on puttin' me back where I came from with wish power,
'cause my show was just gettin' to the good part!
W-Well, I hope you recorded it,
because you're not going anywhere until we get that sword back!
Sword?
Don't play dumb! The Dream Sword!
You're holding it, even!
Oh.
Ohhhh, this sword.
Well, if ya want this so bad...
Here!
You can have it!
whap

What?
Yeah, go on 'n take it!
I got no use fer a fake sword, after all.
Fake?
'S what I just said.
Durn thing don't even come out of the scabbard.
That's—
I-It really doesn't!
Oh no!
So like I said, I got no use fer it.
Cryin' shame, too.
I reckon the real one woulda sold fer a pretty dreampenny.

Wait a second!
How do we know you didn't just make this fake?
Maybe you went and hid the real one somewhere!
What?!
But, Cucumber, what you wished for was the Dream Sword.
This has to be it.
...Oh yeah.
But why won't it come out if it's the real thing?
Hmm...
A-hem.
While we're figurin' that out,
anybody wanna think about sendin' me back home?

I, uh.
Nautilus? How do we send her back?
Hmm...
I suppose...
...you'd have to wait for another shooting star to come by!
What?! That'd take forever!
Y... You could walk.
RRGH!
Now ya done gone 'n made me madder'n a bull in a cape factory!
I sure do hope ya got a weapon other'n that fake sword...
BANG!!
...'cause I'm rarin' to rassle!

AAAAAAAA
Liquus, go!
POW!
Argh! What the—?!
Get offa me!
Great! Now use your—
SQUEEZE

C'mere, ya little—
TUG
YANK
SQUISH
YOINK
There we go!
YEE HAW
Oh NO!
I've got it!
Oh, no ya don't!
H—
Hey!

Yeh heh heh!
Let's see how ya do without this thing!
I-I think we already know.
What do we do?
What can we d-
-huh?
S-Saturday, look out!
There's a UFO headed straight for you!
A what?!
Oh, COME ON, now! Y'all must think I'm dumber'n a sack of—
WHAM

Oh my.
VRRRRRRRR
SSSSSSSSSSSSSSSS
STEP.

A planet under attack!
Its citizens in peril!
A lone cry of distress swallowed whole by the darkness of space...
But WHO will answer it?!
WHO will come forth to defend the defenseless?!
WHO but...
hup!
Commander Caboodle, Champion of Justice!

!!
Justice Log, Entry 5707.
After his sudden crash landing on a distant planet,
the Champion of Justice makes contact with two strange alien creatures.
BUT WAIT! Could they be Dreamsiders?
Judging by those adorable, floppy ears, all signs point to an intergalactic yes!
Greetings, rabbit children!
I am Commander Caboodle (Champion of Justice), and I come in peace.
Greetings, Commander! I am Princess Nautilus.
Um, and I'm Cucumber.

A hearty hello of justice to you...
...Princess Nautilus and Cucumber!
I'm here in search of a dangerous space criminal, and I've got to find my way to a place called...
..."Cake-Town Cast-Le," ASAP.
Caketown Castle?
Oh, this is the Ripple Kingdom!
You'll need to head east to get to where you're going.
Way east...
What?! **Curses!**
And I was **sure** I'd calibrated my navigator perfectly!
OK
Accidents will happen!
They will! **AND DID!**

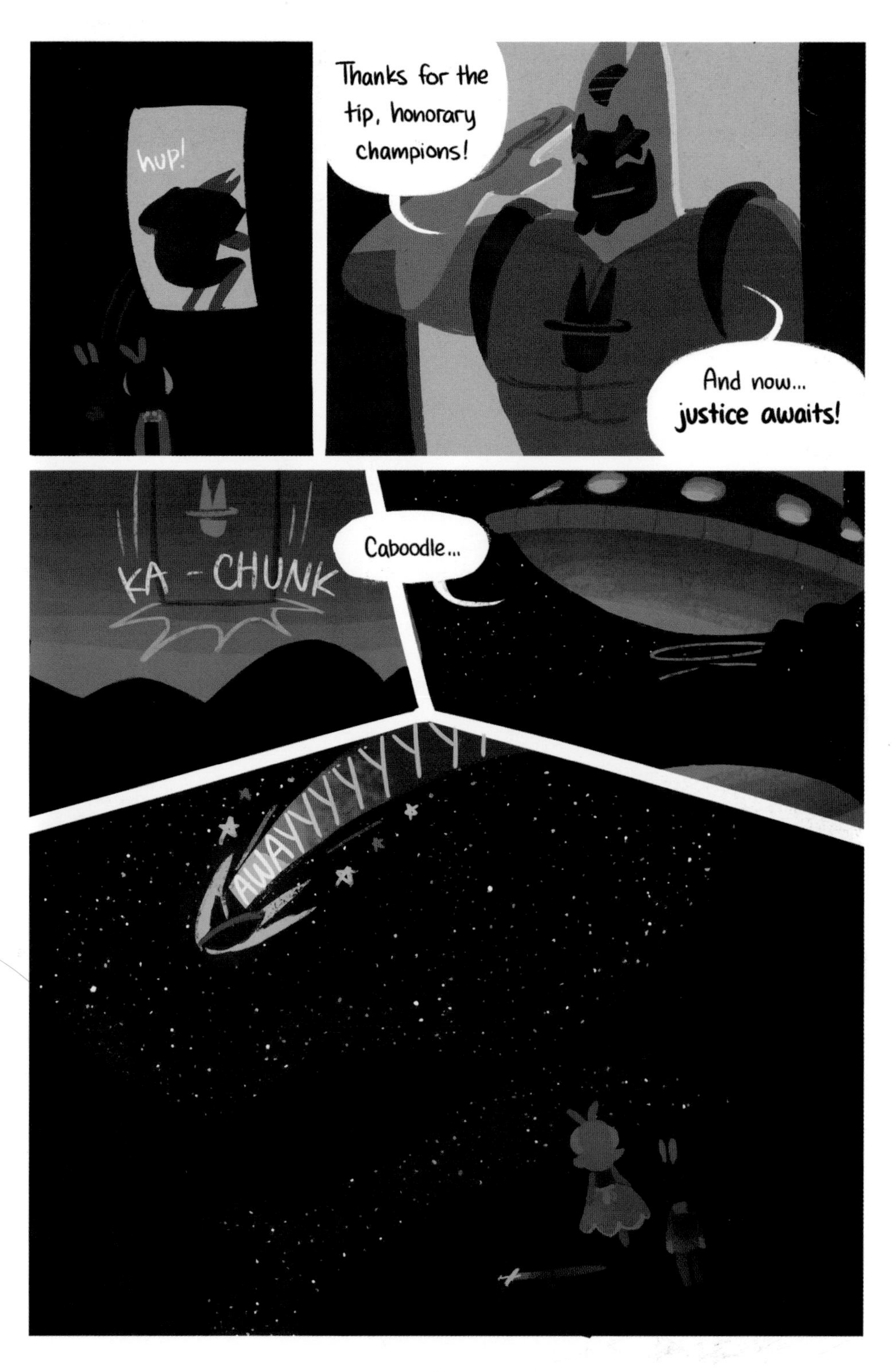
hup!
Thanks for the tip, honorary champions!
And now... justice awaits!
KA - CHUNK
Caboodle...
AWAYYYYYYY!

I wonder what criminal he was searching for.
Caketown Castle...
He must be after Cordelia and the Nightmare Knight, but...
Oh, then that would be good news! He seems very reliable.
...Does he?
heyyyyy
y'allllll
We're almost to Seafoam City, Cucumber. Let's hurry!
R-Right.

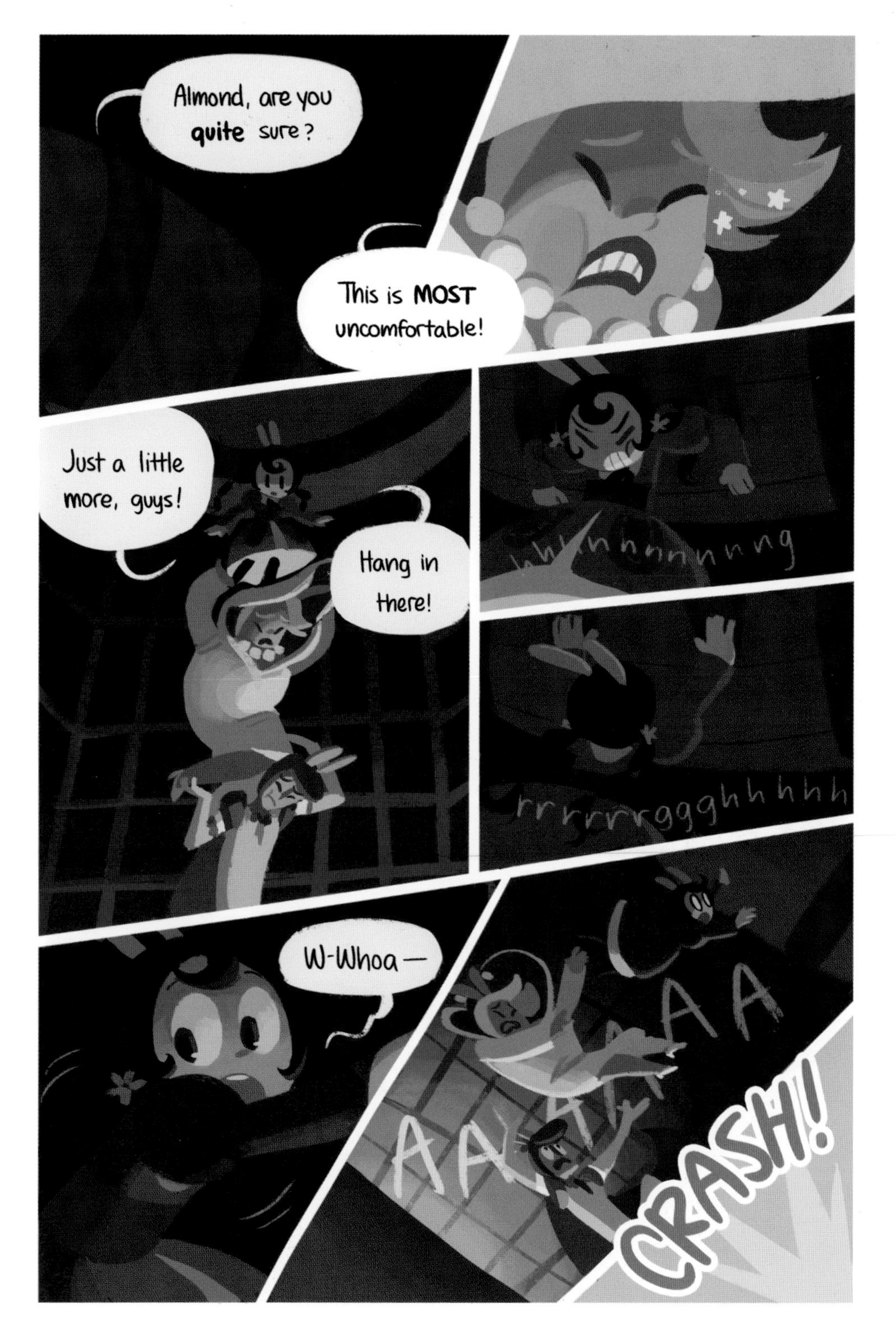
Almond, are you quite sure?
This is MOST uncomfortable!
Just a little more, guys!
Hang in there!
wwnnnnnnng
rrrrrrggghhhhh
W-Whoa—
AAAAAA
CRASH!

A commendable effort, but...
With that barrel over our heads,
I fear our escape may be impossible.
Nuh-uh!
There's gotta be some other way out of this dump!
I'll eat through these bars if I have to!
Don't chew too hard.

Wouldn't want you to break a tooth.
Peridot?!
When Queen Cordelia told me to come see what the Disaster Master was up to,
I thought it might be a fun way to kill time...

But I never dreamed...
...I'd get to see **YOU** trapped like a big, stupid rat!

If you think I'm gonna be stuck in here for long, think again!
Oh, really? So what's your escape plan, genius?
I-I'm working on it, okay?!
Ha ha ha ha!
Knowing Splashmaster will get to finish you off makes me a little jealous, but...
...Actually, it makes me **really** jealous.
Hey!
Get up, dummy!
BUMP

NNNMMMM
GUH?
TINY BUNNY GIRL!
ME SMASH!
Huh?!
SPLASH!!
EEEEK!
What are you doing, stupid?!
I'm on YOUR SIDE!!
OH. ME SORRY.
Ugh!

Just forget it!
Listen, you better beat up this dumb oaf, okay?
S-So I can beat you up later, okay?!
Sure.
Quite the odd girl, isn't she?
No kidding.
Let's come up with a new plan before someone **else** comes to visit!
Right!

Oh no!
My castle!
My city!
Splashmaster did this?
It's even worse than I thought!
We've got to put an end to this, Cucumber!
Let's go inside.

Princess!
You've returned!
We thought you'd been captured by Splashmaster!
I intend to deal with him later!
Are my mother and father all right?
Uh...
King Kelp is safe, but...
Please take me to him!
Y-Yes, Your Highness!

slam!
Father!
Nautilus!
Oh, thank goodness you're safe!
When Splashmaster took you away, I feared the worst!
Where's Mother?
Captured by that awful creature, I'm afraid.
What?!
It was shortly after he'd run off with you,
as if just one kidnapping wasn't dreadful enough.

That does it!
I'm going to defeat Splashmaster and rescue Mother!
On your own?! Insanity!
Oh, gosh, no!
I've found the legendary hero, Cucumber! He's going with me.
R-Right, but
I see!
Well, that's wonderful! A pleasure to meet you, Cucumber.
It gives me hope to see the young hero who will soon rid us of this evil once and for all.
Um...
About that...

What?!
100 times, you say?
How horrible!
But I know there must be a way to defeat him for good!
Right, Cucumber?
Huh?!
Uh...
Right, Your Majesty?
Hmm...
Now that we know, it would be irresponsible for us to allow this cycle to continue.
For the sake of Dreamside's future, we **must** believe there is a way...
even if things seem a bit hopeless at the moment.
Exactly!

For now, though, I think it would be best to focus on defeating the Disaster Masters.
Tell me, have you retrieved the Dream Sword?
Oh!
We have it right here, but...
... it doesn't seem to come out of the scabbard.
We thought you might know why!
Hmm...
Why, Nautilus...
You haven't forgotten your most important duty as the princess, have you?
...I'm sorry, Father. I just couldn't remember that one.
Well, that's perfectly all right, my dear. Everyone forgets things sometimes!
Things they've been studying all their lives?

This sword is the only weapon in our world that can rival the tremendous power of the Nightmare Knight.

It was created with a seal to prevent it from falling into unfit hands.

If you wish to use the Dream Sword in battle,

you must first have it signed by a princess from each of the seven kingdoms.

So that's why Splashmaster's after you!

I can't believe I forgot something so vital!

Let me make it up to you right away.

I shall now perform my greatest duty as princess of this kingdom!

...do you have a marker, or...?

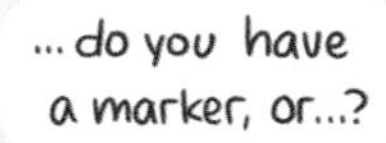

oh i think i might

no, let me

Nautilus
There!
Only six more to go!
"Only"...
That's all well and good,
but surely our brave hero will need a weapon to use against Splashmaster in the meantime.
Our armory should be able to supply you with a sword befitting—
Oh, uh!
I... can't really use a sword, Your Majesty.
You can't?
Actually, my sister's the one who's excited to do all this hero stuff.
Oh!
Then... why are you here?
I-I wish I could tell you that.

I was going to move to the Sky Kingdom to study magic, but some
things
happened.
Magic? Well, that's a different matter entirely!
I don't mean to boast, but I happen to be rather well versed in magic myself.
Really?
My father's the one who taught me how to summon Liquus.
He's really amazing!
Wow!
If you'll just come this way, I have something that might be of use to you on your journey.
I'd be honored!

Take a look, children!
The Extremely Specific and Pretty Much Completely Worthless Capsule Spell Machine!
ESPMCWCSM
the what
Allow me to demonstrate!
Simply turn this crank...
...and out comes a cute plastic capsule!
Oh, I can't take the suspense! Open it!

POP!
Let's see...
"This capsule grants you the power to place a comically oversized bathtub drain on any surface."
ZAP!
Astounding!
what
Now, I have no idea what I might use this spell for.
But a day may come along where I find myself thinking,
"Ohh, if only I had the power to put a gigantic bathtub drain here...!"
...and now, I'll be prepared for that day!
WOW

You try it, Cucumber!
O-Okay...
PUSH
"This capsule grants you the power to place a...
comically oversized bathtub drain on any surface."
Oh.
WOWWW
Two of the same! Incredible!
My boy, with fortune like this,
you're well on your way to joining the Puffington's council one day!
Th- Thank you.

And now...
...it's my turn!
clank!
Pop!
"This capsule grants you the power to order a pizza from anywhere...
...but only when nobody is in the mood for pizza."

I can't think of a single situation where I'd need to use something so pointless.

That's **amazing**, Father!

Isn't it, though?!
HA HA HA HA HA HA HA HA HA HA

Well, I suppose that's all the help I can give you.
Splashmaster's made his lair in Shipwreck Shelter, just beyond here.

This battle may not be an easy one,
but I have faith that the two of you can do it.
So do I!

Are you ready, Cucumber?
W-We wouldn't turn back if I said no, would we?

Farewell, children!
Be careful!
Goodbye!
Thank you!
It's kind of creepy in here...
Stay on your guard, Cucumber. Splashmaster could be anywhere!
Y-Yeah...

A dead end...
Maybe there's a way through underwater?
G-Good thinking!
I'll send Liquus to scout for us!
Call me if you can get through, okay?
NOD
NOD

Stay safe!
He's such a good boy.
Now all we have to do is wait for—
AAAAAA
splish!
Hey, bros.

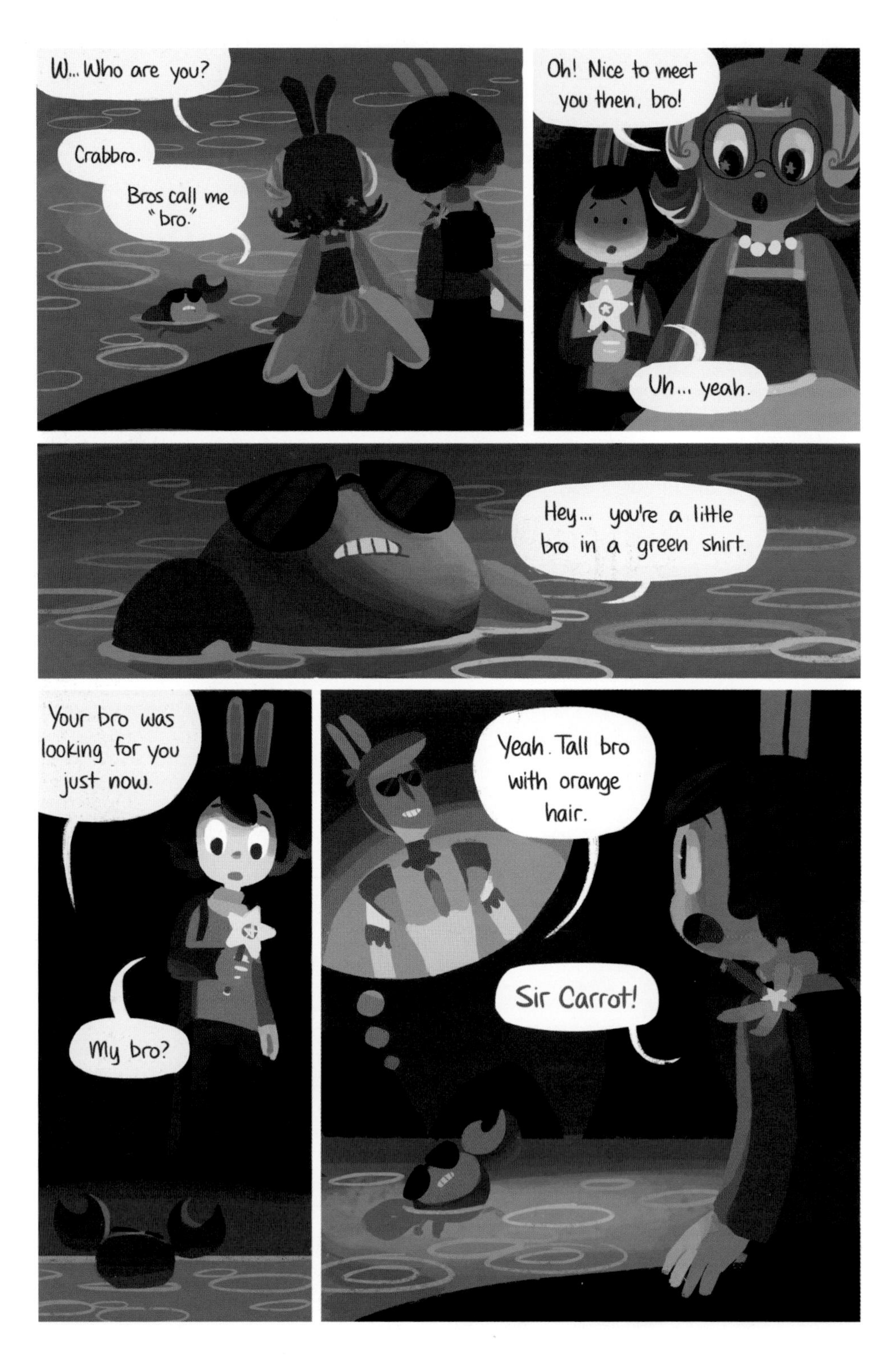
W... Who are you?
Crabbro.
Bros call me "bro."
Oh! Nice to meet you then, bro!
Uh... yeah.
Hey... you're a little bro in a green shirt.
Your bro was looking for you just now.
My bro?
Yeah. Tall bro with orange hair.
Sir Carrot!

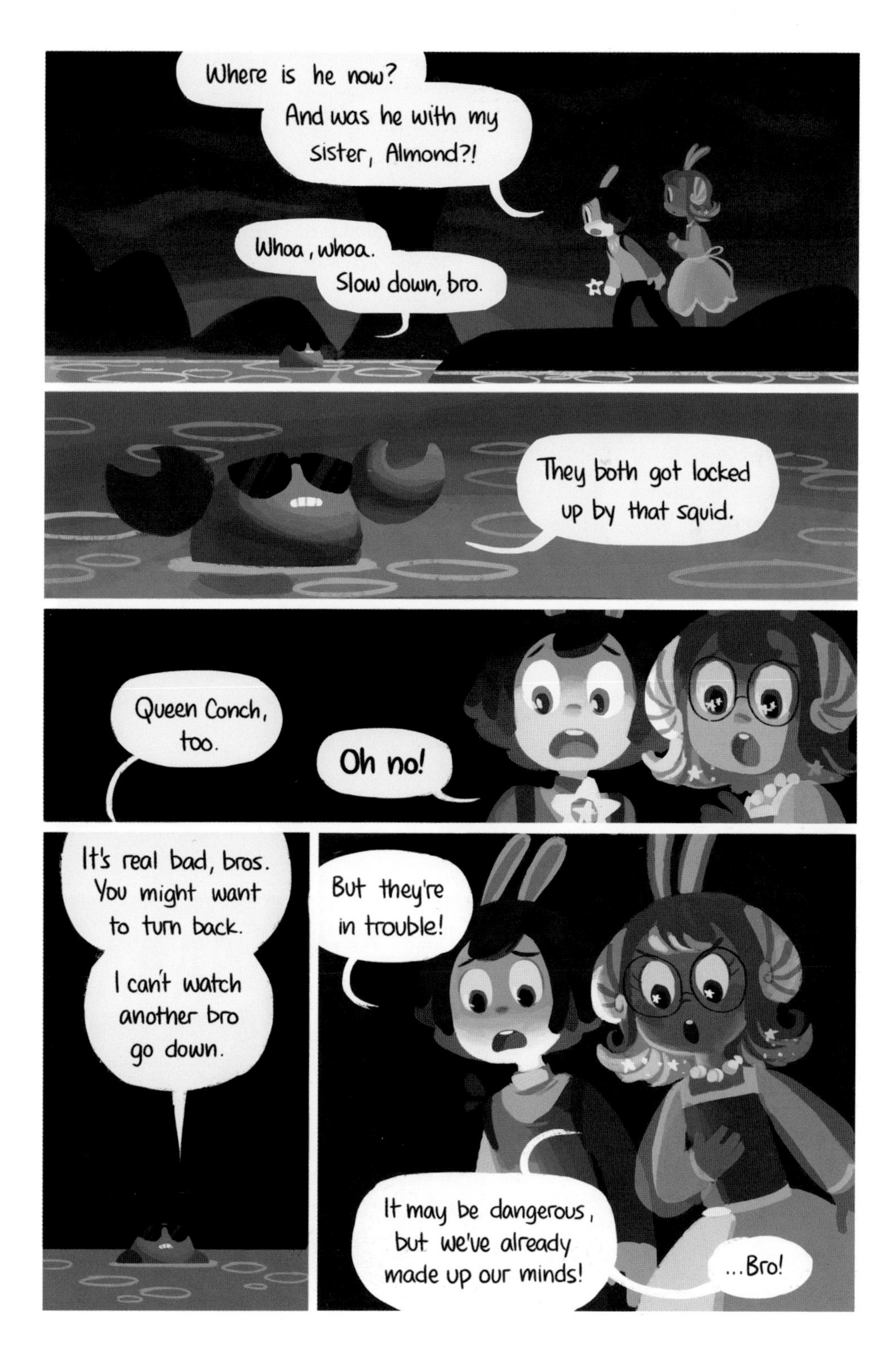
Where is he now?
And was he with my sister, Almond?!
Whoa, whoa.
Slow down, bro.
They both got locked up by that squid.
Queen Conch, too.
Oh no!
It's real bad, bros. You might want to turn back.
I can't watch another bro go down.
But they're in trouble!
It may be dangerous, but we've already made up our minds!
...Bro!

...Okay.
But here's a bro tip.
That squid's place? All water in there.
Not a lot of room for you bros to run around.
I guess we'll have to be careful not to fall in, then.
Y-Yes...
Well, thanks for the tip, um... bro.
Anytime. Good luck, bros.
bloop
Uh-oh...
What's the matter?
I, um... The truth is, I—
AAAAA
DINGA DINGA DING

Does that mean he found a way through?
Y...
Yes! There's an underwater tunnel.
If we swim through that, we'll be in Splashmaster's cave.
Great!
Then let's—
...Nautilus?
I-
I can't—
I can't swim!

Huh?!
Please don't look at me like that, Cucumber. We all have our weaknesses!
B-But your country's covered in water!
And **your** country's covered in **cake**, but I wouldn't expect you to be able to swim through cake!
what
It was a miracle I washed ashore when Splashmaster dropped me, but this is different!
I couldn't possibly hold my breath long enough to make it through!
Oh! Well, if that's all you're worried about, then it's okay.
I have a spell for this!
You do?

I can't hold my breath for very long either, but...
Here!
bloop
As long as you have that, you'll be fine.
Oh!
WOW!
That's incredible, Cucumber!
I-It's really nothing...

Well, what are we still here for?
Let's not keep Liquus waiting!

Oh, what's that?
Huh?
This is...
Almond's sword...
So she really is nearby.
Then let's hurry and return it to her!

splash!
Yayyyyy!
That wasn't so bad, was it?
Not at all! Thank you, Cucumber.
And thank you too, Liquus.
Are we almost there?

splish
Looks like this is it...
Let's go.

Oh!
You guys!
Mother!
Nautilus, darling!
Cucumber!
GUH!
HERO IS HERE! PRINCESS TOO!
NOW ME SMASH BOTH AT ONCE!

NOOOOOOOO!!
HUH?
Nooo!
Whatever you do, PLEEEEASE don't throw a huge barrel at my brother!

go go go go GO GO
HERE ME GOOOOOO!
Uh-oh!
THUD!

AWW, THAT NO WORK.
SPLISH
HEY!
Crud!
UGHHHH!
EEEEK!!

NO RUN!
ME GET HERO LATER. SMASH YOU FIRST!
Good heavens!
Cuco, my sword!
Toss it to me!
O-Okay!
Ready...
Catch!
pft.
Oh, COME ON!

HUH
HUH
TINY BUNNYMAN THROW LIKE **BABY!**
Ugh, stop! You sound like my dad!
HUH HU
HUH H
Ohhh! What shall we do?
nooooo
snap!
OWWW!!

Splash!
Hey, nice one!
I do what I can.
Almond!
Mother!
You're okay!
Oh, I was so worried!
As was I, darling!
But it's all right now.
N-Not quite yet, Your Majesty.
Stay on your guard!

glub glub...
Well, Squidface?
Ready to fight us for real?
Wait a minute!
That's...
LIMBO KING
my limbo crown!

Unbelievable!
Masquerading as limbo royalty this entire time...
How DARE you!
HUH?
THIS CROWN FOR LIMBO?
It says "Limbo King" on it, dude.
OHH.
ME NO CAN READ. JUST WEAR FOR LOOK CUTE.
The GALL!

Uh, Nautilus, I kind of think we have more important things to—
NO, CUCUMBER
oh gosh
This is a matter of pride,
and I will not allow this pretender to make a mockery of my title!
Splashmaster! I, Princess Nautilus, am the true heir to the limbo throne!
Return that crown to me at once!
YOU CRAZY.
ME FIND CROWN. NOW ME KEEP.
Then prove your right to wear it!
I challenge you to a limbo duel!
Huh?

Did someone sayyyyyyyyyyyyyyyyyyyyyyyyyyyyy...
LIMBO?!
HUH?!

Hey, everybody! It's that time again!
Time for the 44th Annual Limbo-thon, that is!
You guys ready to drop 'til you drop?
YEAAAH!!
B-But how—
Then let's get rolling!
Limbo zone, ACTIVATE!
LIMBO

That's right— with this one-of-a-kind Limbo Dimension Generator...

...we're always just one button push away from a party!

But keep in mind that it's a prototype, okay? Real delicate.

So don't go making a ruckus if you lose!

I don't **intend** to lose!

All right, all right, let's get this party **started!**
It's the ultimate battle for limbo supremacy!

YAYYYYYYYYY
Who will claim the crown?!

Yeahh!
Wooo!
Best of luck!
Y-You can do it!
Knock him dead, what's-your-face!

BUT ME NEVER LIMBO BEFORE.
Hmph! Amateur!
What do you say, Princess? Care to show him how it's done?

Watch and learn!
Yowza!
Just look at her go!
That's the kind of skill you'd expect from the Ripple Kingdom's very own **limbo princess!**
But it's not too late for you to nab that crown, Splashmaster!
How low can **YOU** go?!

BUT...
BUT THIS NO FAIR.
What?
Surely you aren't expecting us to raise the limbo pole for you?
BUT IT TOO SMALL!
Lim-bo! Lim-bo! Lim-bo! Lim-bo!
No cheating, Splashmaster!
Are you a limbo king or a limbo commoner?!
LIM-BO!

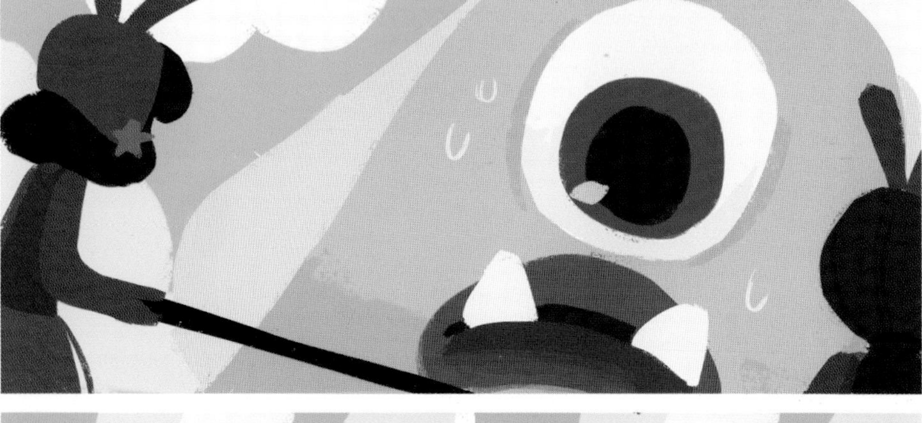

doink

That's it!
We've got our winner, guys!

The limbo queen remains supreme!
YAYYY!
Let's have a big round of applause!
WOOOO!!

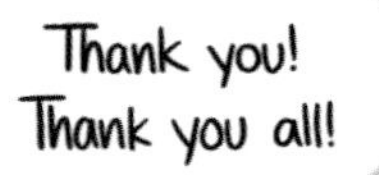
Thank you!
Thank you all!
LIMBO KING
I don't ... think you're supposed to wear it...
GUHH!
THIS NO FAIR!!
CRUNCH
NO!
YOU FOOL!

?
Uh-oh!
SPLASH!

AAAAA
AAAAA!!
AAAAA!!
Stay calm, everyone!
Stay—
OOF!!
EEEEEE
Why's everybody leaving? They're about to miss the good part.
NOOO!!
HEELP!!

You guys!
!
Boing!
Oh no!
I'll handle this!

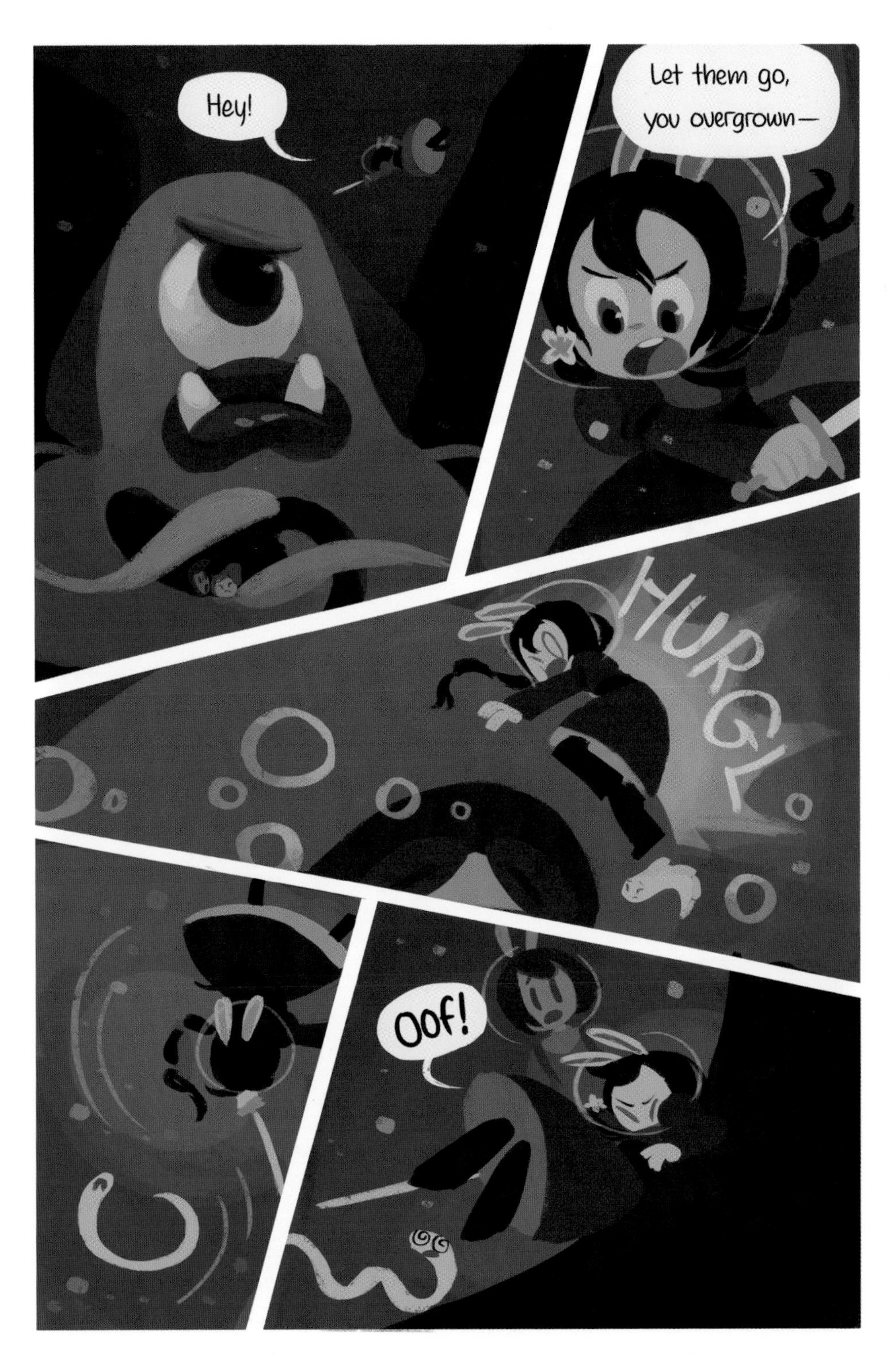
Hey!
Let them go, you overgrown—
HURGL
Oof!

Are you okay?
Ugh! NO.
If he didn't hide underwater like a coward, I could get him!
But how are we supposed to get him OUT of th—
...What?

!
ZAP!
...For real? Where'd you learn how to—
Please just help me pull
glub
glub
glub
glub
glub
glub
drip

HUH??
Sorry, pool's closed!
Or are you too chicken to fight us on dry land?

ME NO NEED WATER!
Too slow!
SLAM
Liquus, hurry!
Now's your chance!

SMACK!
!
VBZZZZZZ
Now we're talking!
Let's get serious!!

THIS is for sinking our boat!
SLICE
And THIS is for kidnapping me!!
WHACK
And THIS is just for being a jerk!!!
And this is...
...for being bad at limbo?
Just finish him off already!

You got it!
I'VEBEENWAITINGFOREVER TOFINALLYGETACHANCETOUSE MYYYYYYYYYYYYYYYYY
EVIL-VANQUISHING
ALMOND SLICER!

GUH!

Greetings, Legendary Hero!
... And other people!

I've come to congratulate you for defeating the first of the Nightmare Knight's minions.
So...
Congratulations!
Only six more to go!
Six, huh? So where's the second one?
You'll find the next of the Disaster Masters in the Melody Kingdom.
And now, I present–
W-Wait!

Is this really the Nightmare Knight's 100th resurrection?
His HUH?!
... So, Chardonnay couldn't keep that little detail to herself, could she?
I don't know what I'm going to do with that girl.
Why keep it a secret?
Oh, use your head, dear.
If I tell a hero the foe he's up against can't be defeated, ever, how do you think he'll react?
He'll lose his nerve, like YOU have!
didn't really have any to start with...
So we're the 100th guys to do this?
And after us will be others...
O Wise Dream Oracle,
isn't there any way to end the cycle?

If I knew how to get rid of him for good, sweetheart, I'd have done it the first time.
The sword may only be a temporary fix, but it's all we have.
But, well... you're the Dream Oracle.
Can't you see the future?
Your point?
I-I mean, couldn't you just tell us if we ever find a way to beat him or not?
Oh, **here** we are.
I was **wondering** when the legendary hero would start telling me how to do my **JOB**.
Um

Do you even understand what you're asking?
What if I gazed into the future...
... only to find Dreamside conquered by the Nightmare Knight and his minions?
How would THAT make you feel?!
Well, it'd be nice to know ahead of ti—
Unthinkable!
We must accept that there are things in this world we are simply not meant to know!
She can't see the future, huh.
I CAN!!

I foresee that you children will create your own future!
Go forth with courage, for only then will you discover the correct path!
Yeah, she totally can't.
Oh, ENOUGH ALREADY!
Here!
I present you with this, the Splash Stone!
Take it as proof of your victory today!

Chapter 1
Good Job!

Thanks to the power of teamwork (and the power of limbo), the heroes managed to defeat Splashmaster.

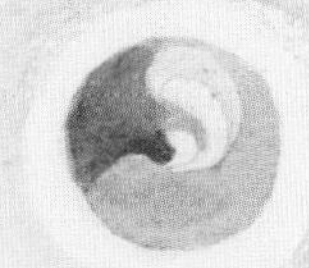

Now, with the first leg of their journey behind them, they set their sights on the Melody Kingdom.

But in light of a new revelation, the future of Dreamside is still uncertain.

And elsewhere, evil forces are already plotting their next move...

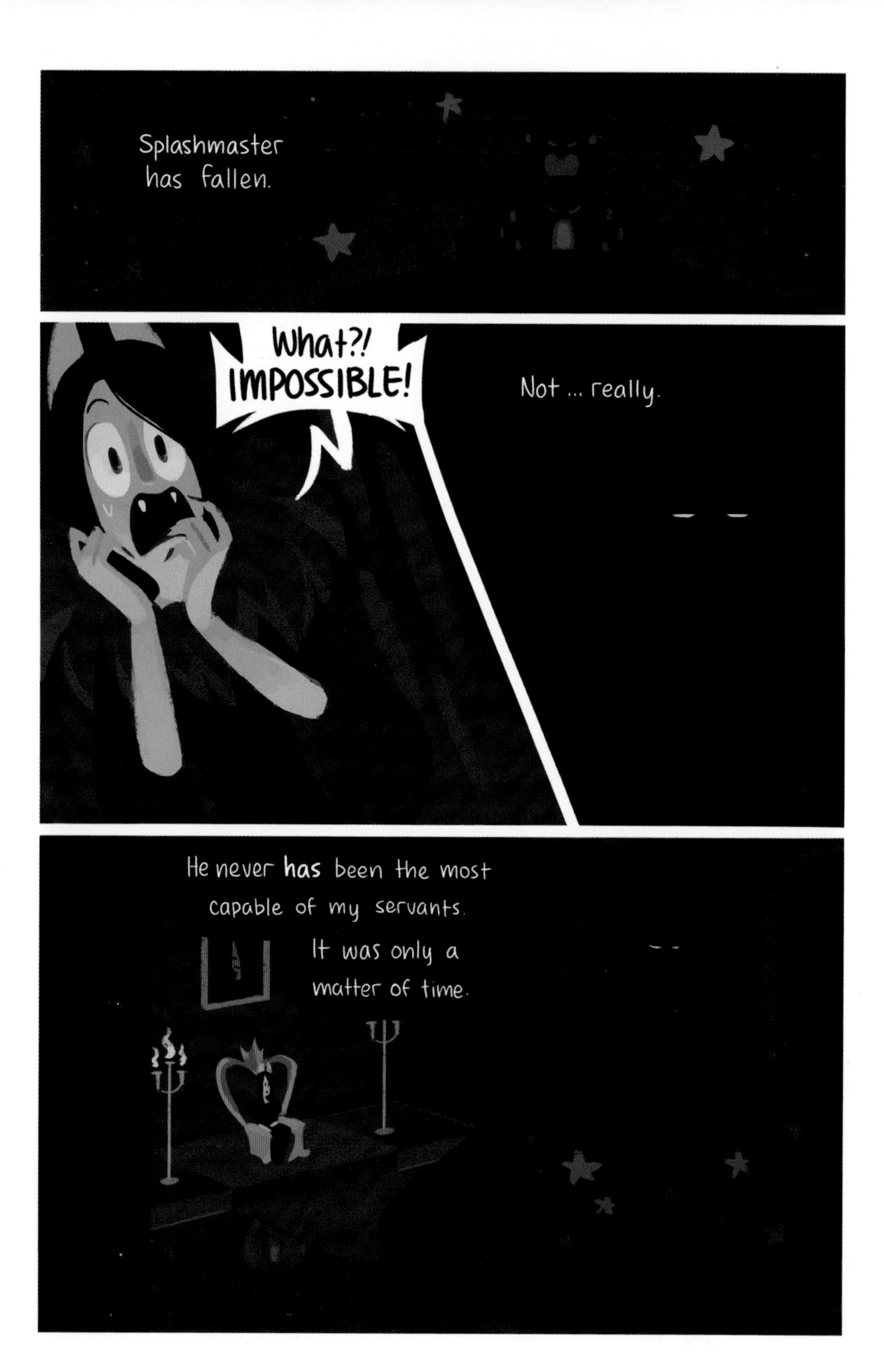
Splashmaster has fallen.
What?! IMPOSSIBLE!
Not ... really.
He never **has** been the most capable of my servants.
It was only a matter of time.

Is that so?
Well, I certainly hope your **other** servants are "capable" of dealing with our hero problem.
Cordelia.
You have done well in resurrecting me.
Know, however, that I am not to be mistaken for one of your subjects.
You would be wise to mind your tone.
O-of course.

The hero and his companions are headed for the Melody Kingdom.
Their journey will end there.
phew
But...
Peridot! Come here!
Whaaat?

Didn't you promise not to call me on Monday nights at 7:30?
I have really important stuff to do then!
Surely no more important than world domination stuff?
Oh, tee hee.
Of course not.
I want you to make preparations to visit the Melody Kingdom, Peridot.
Apparently, our little "hero" and his friends will be there shortly.
So it's finally time for payback, huh?
Got it, Your Majesty!

Hm hm hm...
Excellent.
You may have defeated Splashmaster, Hero, but our battle is only just beginning.
The Doughnut Kingdom is already mine...
...and soon, all of Dreamside will kneel before can we get
rid of that?!
It's really starting to creep me out!

Weren't you the one who wanted it there?
To "celebrate our victory" or whatever?
I think our victory's nice and celebrated by now.
Put this sorry thing in the dungeon, where it belongs!
Fiiine.
C'mon, Gramps.
Anything else?
No, darling. Thank you.

Right down...
Eh?
You're still here?!
The door's unlocked, y'know! We don't actually **need** you for anything.
I dunno, it's kind of cozy down here.
Maybe I'm gettin' old.

Whatever.
Say hi to your new cellmate.
hmm...
Looks just like a guy I used to work for!
Ha HA!!!

W-
What are you doing out here?
Oh. Peridot.
Peridot
ˈpɛrɪ ˌdɒt

Okay, I know you're all scary and invincible and stuff,
so I'm gonna let it slide this time,
but for future reference? It's "Peri - DOH."
Silent "T"! Got it?!
...I hadn't realized it was so important.
OF COURSE it's important!!
How would you like it if I said YOUR name wrong,
Mr. Nightmare Knit?!

Oh! Jeez, what am I still here for?!
I'm gonna miss the end!
Laterrr!!
NOOO

Arrêeete!
Quiet down, Princess!
You want the whole castle to hear, or what?
The whole COUNTRY will 'ear if you don't give that back!
Oh! You mean...
...THIS old thing?!
Gee, I don't know... Something about the design just bugs me.

I mean, listen—I'm no fashion expert...
...but I just don't think it complements your **exquisite beauty.**
Like, for sure! Tacky City!
And it's **orange!**
It's beautiful to me, and that's all that matters!
Give it BACK!
Well, I guess we **could** make some kind of arrangement.
Say, one ugly necklace in exchange forrr...
one smooch?!

Dégoûtant!
I'd rather kiss a pig!
Whoops!
Man, I'm such a butterfingers today!
NO!
Please, you can't!
Pathetic.

Like, ohmygosh!
When I heard that insufferable screaming, I expected a waste of my time...
...but this is almost insulting.
H-Huh? What's your deal, buddy?
In case you didn't know, watching the princess's room is my job.
So it is.
If you intend to keep it, return to your post.

You've got a lot of nerve, acting like you own this place already!
Let me tell you something, pal: what I do is none of your business!
So unless you want trouble,
I **suggest** you make like a banana and splohhhhhHHH MYGOOOSH
PUT ME DOWN PUT ME DOWN
FEET ON GROUND PUT FE

OOF!
!!!
H-Here!
Take your stupid necklace back!
Let's scraaam!

Wait!
Please!
Th-
Thank you!
shut.

And so, the time has come for us to say goodbye.
You've done phenomenal work, children!
We are in your debt.
Please, Your Majesties, think nothing of it!
Yeah! It's just part of the job.
Thanks for, um, everything, Your Majesty.
And thank you too, Nautilus!
I bet I'd still be stranded on the beach if you hadn't been there.
Oh no!
I should be thanking you! I, um...
Um.

This Nightmare Knight business has us all feeling uneasy about what lies ahead...

...but I have faith that if the four of you work together,

you'll find a way to save Dreamside for good.

You must let me know if the food in other kingdoms is as good as I've been told!

uh

But you must also lend your strength to our legendary heroes.

Help these young people triumph over the Nightmare Knight one last time!

The Royal Sea Train was heavily damaged by Splashmaster,
but under the guidance of our new engineer, repairs went exceptionally well.
Ah, and now the time has come for us to **really** say goodbye.
Take care, children!
Byeeee!

shhhhhhhhhhhh

18th, year ♥♪☺○☆

Travel Log 30

My companions and I have set out for the Melody Kingdom, where we shall seek the aid of the fair Princess Piano. Rumor has it that the princess' songs are the most beautiful in all of Dreamside, but I laugh at such rumors! What sound in this world is more angelic than the voice of Princess Parfait?

18th, ♥♪☺○☆

Dearest Diary,

Mother and Father allowed me to leave home today. This is a journey of great importance, and the fate of our world hangs in the balance...

but I'm **SO EXCITED!**

I can't wait to see the Melody Kingdom! I wonder how Princess Piano is doing.

UGH! I can't believe the bad guy's been brought back to life 100 times! Where's the fun in this epic quest thing if 99 other dorks beat me to it already??

I guess I just have to be the first hero to do it right, huh? I bet the ~~Knt~~ Nightmare ~~Night~~ Knight isn't even that tough if he's lost so many times!

18th,

I still don't think I'm a hero, but if it means people in the future won't have to worry about the Nightmare Knight anymore, I think I want to do what I can to keep him from coming back. Maybe one day, there will be someone like me who can go to school if they want to!

...I kind of wish I knew what to do, though...

C'mooooon!
Are we theeeere yeeeet?!
Not for a few more hours!
And—hey, stop that!
The Sea Train truly is a marvel, Your Highness.
Isn't it?
It's a shame we'll have to wait another hour for breakfast, though.
Indeed. I must say, I'm quite famished.
Knock Knock
Snack caaart!

Oh, how convenient!
Good heavens!
Whoa!
Look at all of this!
Help yourselves.

Hee, hee.
Hi again.
W-What are **YOU** doing here?
Well, now! Is that any greeting for the person who got you to the Ripple Kingdom safe and sound?
"Safe and sound," my butt!
Your faulty invention nearly cost us our **lives**!
"Faulty"...?
You must be mistaken. The S.S. Cosmo was flawless.

It **stopped** in the middle of the ocean!
It was a solar-powered vehicle.
What did you expect it to do with no sun?
But how could we have known about the storm?
Well, that was an unfortunate coincidence.
I think we've all learned a valuable lesson about checking the weather forecast before embarking on perilous overseas journeys.

I'll teach
YOU A LESSON!
Almond!
You know...
That giant squid monster destroying my ship was as heartbreaking for me as I'm sure it must have been for you.
I-I don't think heartbreak is the issue here.
But since the
test
was such a success,
I don't mind that I've lost a good invention in the process.
J-Just what—
Have a muffin!
You've earned it.

You still haven't told us.
What are you doing here?
Hee.
Why wouldn't I be on this train, Cucumber?
I'm DRIVING IT!!
NO

The Sea Train is a work of art, but it's a bit...

behind the times, in my opinion.

Hee, hee.

Then allow me to convince you.

Observe.

Computer! Speed up the train, please!
...
beep!
COMMAND RECOGNIZED:
"Blow up the train, Plea
I can do that for you
"BLOW UP THE TRAIN"
ACTIVATING DETONATOR
Oh.
Oops.
WHAT
Y-You put a **bomb** on the train?!
Maybe.
Are you **CRAZY?!**
I've been called that.

Well!
15:00
ESCAPE
As fun as this reunion has been,
I really should be going.
I wish there were enough room for all of you on this emergency escape platform, but, well.
Oops.
COSMO!!
You'll just need to find that bomb yourselves! But that should be no trouble for you, right?
Good luck, friends!
Wait!
UGH!!

W-What shall we do?!
We've no time to search the entire train!
beep
beep
beep
beep
14:19 31
M-Maybe if we start in the engine room or some—
Oh my!
Huh?
That isn't Cosmo, is it?
That's...!
AHEH HEH HEH
HEH HEH HEH
No way!
HEH

Yeh heh heh!
Hope y'all weren't fixin' to get away easy after what ya done in the Ripple Kingdom!
Hit 'em, Brambleby!
POW!
SMAK
Howdy, passengers! We're hoppin' aboard,
so make it easy fer everybody 'n start emptyin' them pockets!
Why **now**?!

Hooo-wee!
I've been itchin' fer some new riches, Brambleby...
...and this fancy-pants train is ripe fer the pickin'!
You're gonna have to deal with us first, Saturday!
Oh! I was waitin' fer y'all to come on out.
Brambleby?
Whoa, what?!
SWIPE

I gotta run.
Y'all have fun, now!
slam!
Just us, huh?
Didn't really think you were the fighting type.
flip
flip
Only if Saturday orders it.
...You know, it's a lot harder to talk to you without signs on the walls.
flip
flip
flip
flip
I couldn't find my whiteboard.
Oh.

09:59 01

We've no time to waste, Your Highness!

We **must** find that explosive!

Let's leave no stone unturned!

SLICE!
WOOP
REALLY?!
How many brooms do you have?!
H-He really takes his job seriously, huh?
He's just wasting our time!
If they don't find that bomb soon, we're—
Done!!

Hoo!
Got us a dang fortune, Brambleby!
!!
Time to skedaddle!
Wh—you can't just—!
Bye, now!
Better luck next time!
Get back here!
thump
thump
thump
thump
We've found it!

The bomb!
N-Now we just need to figure out how to deact—
Oh,
gimme that!
HEH HEH HEH HE
Huh?!
THUNK

KABOOOOM!!
THIS AIN'T OVERRRRRR
OH NOOO

Way to go, Almond!
What'd you expect?
And you guys did great, too!
Where'd you find the bomb?
HOMF
SNOMF
SLURP
SLURP
You guys?

Hey, look!
Isn't that it?

To be continued in...
Cucumber
QUEST
3

Reader questions for...
Almond & Cucumber!
"Q" Almond, that final attack was the coolest!
I know, right?!
It's just like Punisher Pumice's Pretty Pumice Power Punisher!
I spent months practicing at home!
Y-You can still see the evidence in our backyard.
I still feel like it was missing something, though.
Like what?
A good one-liner, you know?
If you say the right thing just before you finish the bad guy off, it makes your attack sooo much cooler!
Pumice does it all the time!

I should have been like,
"Time to get a tenta-clue."
I'll have a good one for next time.
Pff
Cucumber, you've never seen or met the Nightmare Knight; what do you think he's like?
I-I'm trying not to think about that...
I mean, if I imagine the Nightmare Knight as a scary legend instead of an actual villain we actually have to fight at some point,
it makes me feel a little bit better about this whole thing.
I met him!
Want me to—
NO PLEASE

Q Cucumber- I know your sister is into Punisher Pumice, but what TV shows do you like?
Um, I don't watch very much TV, but when I do, it's usually history shows and stuff like that.
Oh, actually, the last thing I saw before we left home was a biography special about Cumulo Puffington.
here he goesss
H-He's my role model!
Aside from being the founder of the academy, Mr. Puffington has made so many important magical discoveries.
People consider him the greatest wizard in Dreamside, but he also seems like a really kind person...
I really look up to him, so it'd be amazing to meet him one day.
Gonna have him sign the poster in your room?
Don't tell them about that!!

Q Almond! Were you ever bullied in school? Was your brother bullied?
Yeah, kids at school bullied Cuco for about a day before I set 'em straight.
Now they know better.
Almond's like a really scary hall monitor.
It's basically knight training!
I wish I could say she scared off all the bullies at school, but...
1 year ago...
Oh nooo, where'd I put my—
shuffle
shuffle
Lunch money tax!
!!
Pay up, squirt!
NOooooo
Left your book report on the kitchen counter, son.
th-thanks, dad

Reader questions for...
Carrot & Nautilus!
Q Carrot, why did you become a knight?
Why, out of a profound desire to serve my king and country, of course!
For what other reason does one become a knight?
Looking cool and getting in fights?
For shame, Almond!
A proper knight must use her strength for the sole purpose of protecting—
Look, knights wear cool uniforms, right?
W-Well, er, I suppose you might-
And they get in fights, right?
Erm... on occasion, b—
Next question!

Q Sir Carrot, what was it like serving as a knight before disaster struck the kingdom?
Before the Nightmare Knight's resurrection, the Doughnut Kingdom was a land of peace and prosperity.
Guess you didn't have a lot to do then, huh?
On the contrary, I had many daily responsibilities!
Nothing quite matches the thrill of rescuing stray pets and massaging His Majesty's feet!
He really means that, doesn't he.
I think so.

Q Nautilus, how did you meet Liquus?
This Royal Instrument of Summoning was a birthday gift from my mother and father years ago.
Your personality determines the familiar you summon, so Liquus and I were meant for each other from the start!
Hey, that's pretty cool!
hee hee
I wonder what kind of familiar I'd get.
Something cute, I think!
Sure, but it'd have to be pretty tough, too.
Oh, certainly.
But I'm sure it'd have a soft side.
MOM
Why not!

Q Nautilus, what tips can you give an up-and-coming limbo novice?

Anyone can simply limbo, but only through years of physical and mental discipline can one become a true master. It is **not** for the faint of heart.

I am prepared, milady!

Your humble pupil awaits instruction.

Wonderful!

Then I'll share the forbidden training technique I used as a beginner!

BZZZZZRT

If you can limbo under this, you can limbo under anything!

Go on!

GO ON, MY DISCIPLE

Reader questions for...
Bacon!
Q why
Huh? Why what?
If you're asking why lollipops always get those hard edges that cut your tongue when you lick them too long, I dunno...
... but I asked Sir Tomato once, and he got really mad—
NUH-UH!!
I haven't gotten to answer a single question yet, and there's NO WAY I'm losing my spot AGAIN!
DO IT OVER!!

Reader questions for...
Peridot & Cordelia!
That's better!
Q Peridot, do you have any siblings?
NO.
Q Hey, Peridot, what do you really think of our "heroes"?
She's dumb!
I-I mean THEY'RE dumb!!
UGGGHHH, why am I getting all the dumb questions?!
There, there.
Q Peridot, why did you learn magic?
So I could boss people around? Duh. Why does anybody learn magic?
WH—

But I'm kind of a natural prodigy, so it's not like I had to study.

Impressive. No magic school?

Definitely no magic school.

Who goes there but losers?

WH

Q Queen Cordelia, who is your ideal man?

That's the problem with being as powerful, gorgeous, and cunning as I am. There **are** no men who could hope to stand at my side.

...But let's be honest. It isn't like Caketown has very much in the way of boyfriend material.

What about the Nightmare Knight?

I'm not **that** old yet.

hee hee
Sorry!
But I bet you have a dream boyfriend, right?
Hm, let me think...
Handsome, intelligent, rugged, daring...
GET OUT!
WINK!

Princess Nautilus

Atk ★
Def ★★★★
Sp ★★★★

R.I.S.
fishy earrings
rose-tinted glasses

Every heroic quest needs some positive energy, and the Ripple Kingdom princess has more than enough to spare. No trial is too daunting, no enemy too great, no, uh...

How did the rest of that go? I forget.

Splashmaster

Atk ★★★★★+
Def ★★
Sp ★

While he may be the first, and therefore the weakest, of the Nightmare Knight's seven henchmen, Splashmaster's physical strength is nothing to sneeze at. It's just too bad he doesn't have the smarts to match.

Chardonnay

Atk ★
Def ★
Sp ★

- the Oracle's coffee
- the Oracle's laundry
- an unbreakable spirit

The Dream Oracle's hapless devotee and personal assistant. Chardonnay wants nothing more than to be helpful, and she won't give up no matter what! But has she ever considered that her job might be getting in the way...?

King Kelp

Atk ★
Def ★
Sp ★★★★★

- octo-stick
- history book
- spell capsule

Ruler, father, scholar, and goofball. Upon meeting him, one wonders if Queen Conch is the only grounded member of the family.

But, hey, at least they have fun.

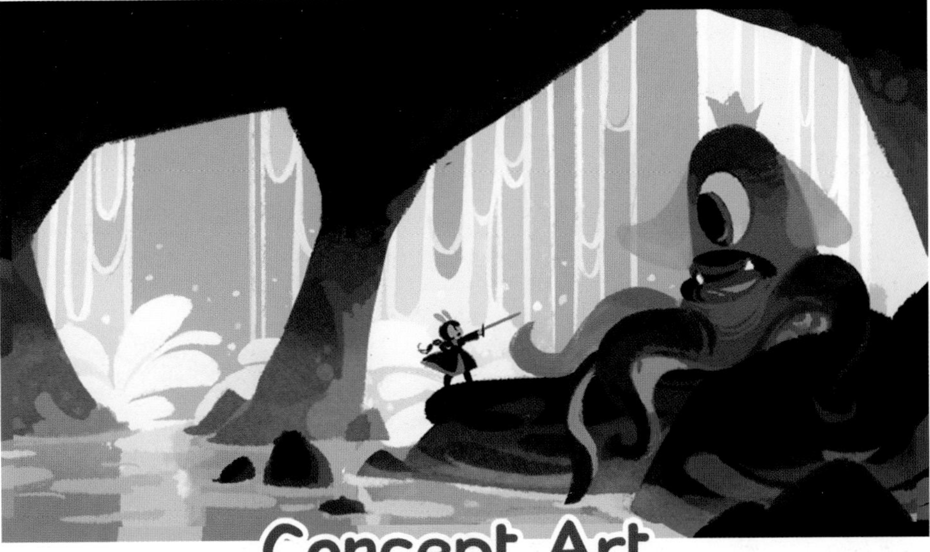

Concept Art

WELCOME

SPLASHMASTER

welcome to the

Ripple Kingdom!

Greetings!

You may think you've seen everything the Ripple Kingdom has to offer, but you haven't had a proper tour yet. If you're thinking about a vacation, please allow me to be your guide!

Pack a swimsuit!

Make it cute, see?

Pack a camera!

For capturin' memories and whatnot, see?

Pack sunscreen!

...Do bunny people need this?

Think it's impossible for just anyone to get a room at the ultra-exclusive, extra-extravagant

...Well, yeah, it kind of is. With its five-star service and gorgeous accommodations, it's no wonder every VIP in Dreamside stays there.

But if you get a chance to eat at the restaurant, Chef Crabcake's seaweed pasta is to die for!

By the way...

Bubblebeard, who founded the resort twenty years ago, is an ex-pirate captain...which might explain why he runs such a tight ship.

Apparently, Captain Bubblebeard met my father during one of his expeditions, and it was after they became friends that he decided to settle down and start a business.

I wonder if they went on any exciting voyages together...?

Seafoam City

The Ripple Kingdom's capital may have been wrecked by Splashmaster recently, but it's usually a beautiful, lively place. Why not see for yourself?

...What's that? How did it get repaired so quickly, you ask?

Did you know that Seafoam City is home to one of the largest magic libraries in the world? While it's not quite on par with Puffington's Academy, it still draws scholars from all over.

We do have the largest aquarium, though!

Citizens and tourists alike have nothing to fear, as King Kelp's fiercely loyal sea horse knights uphold peace on the city streets!

(...Okay, so maybe they weren't much help against Splashmaster, but they usually do a pretty good job. You should have seen them escorting people to safety!)

Hey, no complaints about the uniform! Can I keep this one?

Before you head home, be sure to stop by...

This stargazing spot, loved by romantic poets and philosophers for millennia, is one of Dreamside's top tourist attractions.

You already know this, but any wish made on a shooting star reflected in the lagoon's magical waters will be granted instantly. The chances of it happening are pretty low, but still...what would you wish for?

"The safety of our darling Nautilus and her friends."

"Peace for every bro."

And my wish is for you to return to our kingdom very soon!

See you again!

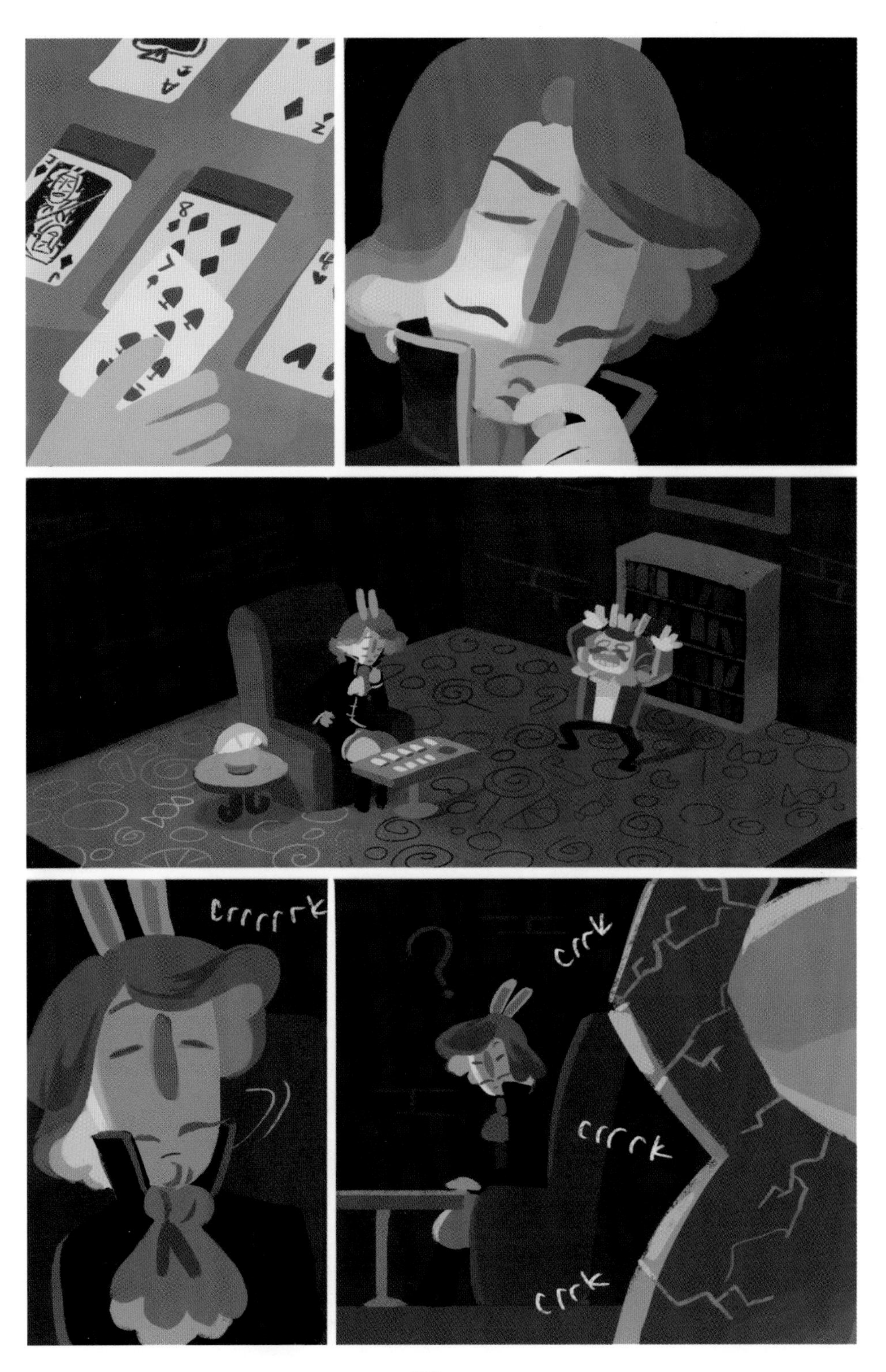
Crrrrrk
crrk
crrrk
crrk

CRASH!!
OUF!
Well, hey!
Would you look at that.
Cabbage? Is zat you?
One and only.
Mais, where **is** zis place?!
What 'as 'appened to us?!
Whoa-ho, Chief! Calmez-vous!
We're in the dungeon.
Cordelia tossed us in here after she took over Caketown.
QUOI?!

Boy, you don't remember anything, do you?
And Parfait? Where is she?!
Locked up somewhere, apparently.
SACRE-BLEU!
'Ow could zis 'appen?!
Ze kingdom is lost...
Ma petite ange, a prisoner...
Sniff
sniff
Et vous, Cabbage?
What are you doing in all of zis chaos?
Me?
Well, I'm playing solitaire, but we can make this Go Fish, easy.

IMBÉCILE!
Now is ze time for ACTION!
We must make ze escape, tout de suite!
Yeah!
But 'OW?!
THERE's that 7!
Ah, ze bars!
Per'aps I can...
Zut alors!
Suck it in, Boss!
Squeeeeeak!

Zis is not defeat!
We must dig ze TUNNEL!
Vite, Cabbage! I need quelque chose for ze digging!
Sorry, left my shovel at home.
I-In zat case, I 'ave...
...NO CHOICE!
flop
Listen, Your Majesty, just because it's candy...
SLUUURP

If it is to save mon ange...
...I will throw away ze dignity!
Oh, ma pauvre Parfait...
I cannot 'ave ze peace until I know zat you—
CREEE
eeeeeeeeeeeak
are
safe
Door's open, by the way.

I want a caaaaake.
Oh? Why not go and terrorize the local bakeries like usual?
I don't feel like going ouuut.
What kind of castle **is** this, anyway?
Aren't we supposed to have, like, **cooks** or something?
You **did** turn them all to—
Squeak!
Oh.

Oh **my**.
So the spell **isn't** permanent after all.
Yeah, well, I never said it **WAS**.
Oh, don't be offended, dear.
I think all His Former Majesty needs is a second helping.
That I can do!

Non, non, NON!! Please, 'ave mercy!
To see ma Parfait, zat is all I want!
Sooo-rry, the princess isn't seeing anybody today.
Or ever.
Oh, but I am begging you! I will do ANYTHING!
Cry me a river, Grandp-
...Anything anything?
Euh...

Thank you for reading!

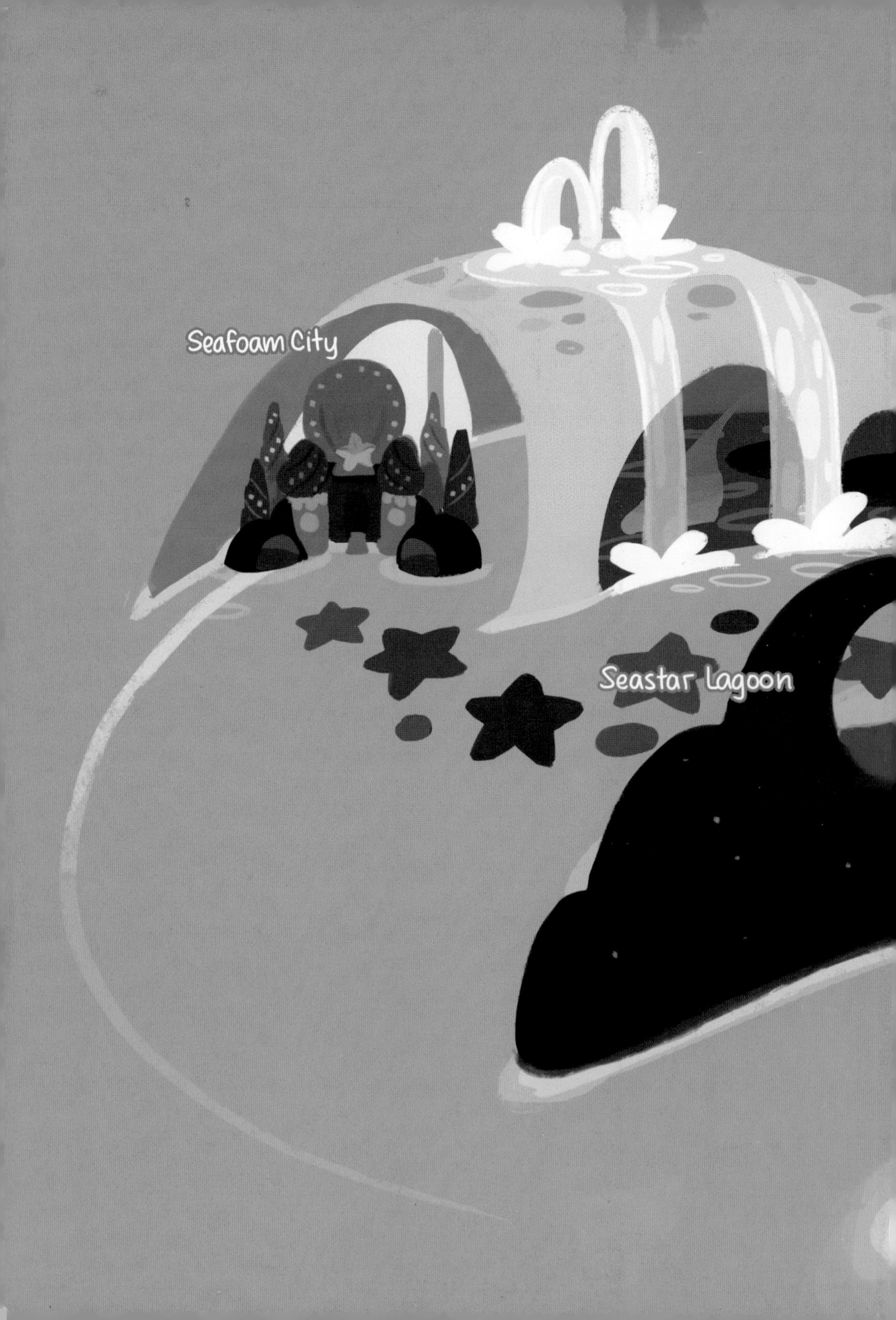
Seafoam City
Seastar Lagoon

The Ripple Kingdom
Shipwreck Shelter
Coral Canyon
Bubblebeard Beach
LIMBO
Crabster Resort

:01
First Second
New York

Published by First Second
First Second is an imprint of Roaring Brook Press, a division of
Holtzbrinck Publishing Holdings Limited Partnership
120 Broadway, New York, NY 10271

Library of Congress Control Number: 2017941161

Hardcover ISBN: 978-1-25015-982-3
Paperback ISBN: 978-1-62672-833-2

Our books may be purchased in bulk for promotional, educational, or business use. Please contact your local bookseller or the Macmillan Corporate and Premium Sales Department at (800) 221-7945 ext. 5442 or by e-mail at MacmillanSpecialMarkets@macmillan.com.

First edition 2018
Book design by Rob Steen

Cucumber Quest is created entirely in Photoshop.

Printed in China by RR Donnelley Asia Printing Solutions Ltd., Dongguan City, Guangdong Province.

Hardcover: 10 9 8 7 6 5 4 3
Paperback: 10 9 8 7 6